COMPROMISING POSITIONS

The ugly death of a pretty upstairs maid had put the chief of the Paris police in a most embarrassing position. But if he hadn't killed her, who had?

Roland, Duke of Charanton—Lorette's influential uncle. He could wield enormous power, but would he end his niece's humiliation by murder?

Henri Bayard—The rheumy-eyed old chauffeur at the manor. He had promised his service to M. le Chef, but had he also sworn a vow of vengeance?

M'sieu Poidevin—A wealthy neighbor of M. le Chef. Once he had held a position of great prominence. Why was he now a recluse in Pontlieu?

Lorette—The beautiful blue-eyed wife of M. le Chef. Her husband flaunted his infidelity, but was she capable of bashing in her rival's head?

The clever—and quite married—M. Pinaud swore to solve this mysterious affair of the heart, but would his own be broken as he proceeded to *cherchez la femme*?

Murder Ink.® Mysteries

Scene of the Crime® Mysteries

A Scene Of The Crime® Mystery

AND ONE FOR THE DEAD

Pierre Audemars

A DELL BOOK

Published by
Dell Publishing Co., Inc.
1 Dag Hammarskjold Plaza
New York, New York 10017

Dell ® TM 681510, Dell Publishing Co., Inc.

ISBN: 0-440-10442-4

Reprinted by arrangement with Walker and Company
Printed in the United States of America
First Dell printing—January 1983

To
Josette Rochat

One law for a living man
And another law for the dead

A. C. Swinburne: *A Lamentation*

1

In the days when all the new and incomprehensible changes in a hitherto familiar world caused M. Pinaud not only dismay but concern and even distress, he nevertheless derived considerable comfort from the consoling thought that the first principles on which he had been brought up to base his conduct and order his life still remained unchanged, inviolate, and with even greater strength and validity than ever before . . .

To one of his nature, this was a pleasing thought, and one to which he often returned in times of stress and depression. The obligations of friendship, for example, had always been to him clear-cut and definite. Otherwise the word had no meaning.

He remembered very vividly the time M. le Chef had been in trouble . . .

One might truthfully say that it really began on the morning of that same day he received the midnight telephone call, when he stood respectfully to attention in the beautiful room of M. le Chef on the first floor, his request for an interview having been graciously accorded.

M. le Chef contemplated the single sheet of virgin paper which lay exactly in the centre of his blottingpad with a faint distaste—as if its very presence implied connotations that were vaguely unpleasant—and then looked up.

'Ah yes—Pinaud. You wished to see me?'

'Yes, m'sieu,' replied M. Pinaud promptly—since M. le Chef was obviously a busy man—and yet carefully without too much eagerness. 'It is about my car.'

'And what about your car, Pinaud?'

The very wording of the phrase, quite apart from its tone should have warned him, but it was not in his nature to hesitate or prevaricate, once his mind had been made up and the decision taken. He continued rapidly, trying to speak concisely and factually. This was not easy, since it was a subject on which he felt very deeply.

'I do not have to tell you, m'sieu, how pleased I am
with my present car and how proud I am of it. There is
no one in the whole organization who looks after his car
in the way I care for mine. I have made no secret of my
feelings towards it. To me a car is so much more than a
piece of machinery. I accept the fact that since it moves
it must be alive. Mine is a living thing. On long and lonely
trips I talk to it. After a particularly difficult and hazardous
journey, when by its performance it has undoubtedly saved
my life, I have been known to thank it. On one occasion,
when I had been singing—in order to try to cut down on
my smoking—I definitely heard a noise from the back, in
tune, in unison and in answer. Indeed, I could almost say,
quite truthfully, that—'

Here, having become aware of the expression on M. le
Chef's face, he checked himself abruptly and swallowed
whatever he had been about to say quite truthfully. He
took a deep breath and came down to earth.

'I have not told you these things, m'sieu, as idle gossip
to waste your valuable time or to bore you, but to impress
upon you the magnitude of my decision. The point is that
the car is getting old and—whatever my feelings—I need
and must have a new one. I have already had several minor
breakdowns on the road. I have kept this car long over the
regulation replacement period and to continue driving for
any more of the great distances I have to travel in the
course of duty would be not only uneconomical, but posi-
tively—'

'No,' interrupted M. le Chef, coldly and clearly and
calmly.

'But—'

'I said no. No to your request. No new car. That should
be quite clear.'

M. Pinaud swallowed. Not only saliva, but bile and
frustration and anger and bitterness and resentment as
well. This was the last thing he had expected.

'May I ask why—'

'Naturally. You have made a reasonable request. This
has been refused. It is your right to ask for an explanation.

As much your right, Pinaud, as it is my duty to give you the reasons.'

M. le Chef paused and placed his fingertips together in front of his face. He stared down through the arch of his hands, with what had become now a positive dislike, at the unoffending piece of paper.

'The reason is basically one of economy' he continued quietly. 'At the moment this establishment simply cannot afford the expense of a new car, whatever the justification. Behind this reason, Pinaud, there are other reasons which have caused it. You are fully entitled to my confidence, and therefore you shall have it.'

His hands suddenly clenched and gripped together in a gesture that was startling in its intensity.

'There are very powerful influences at work these days trying to get me out—out of this chair, this room and this building.'

M. Pinaud looked at him incredulously.

'But I always thought that the Minister was a friend—'

'He was. M'sieu le Ministre Poidevin. He still is a friend. You met him yourself. The case of the Krontine diamonds, do you remember? He praised you as incorruptible. But now he is only M'sieu Poidevin. He has retired. He has no influence and no power. He is a private citizen. His successor is a swine. I think he has ideas of setting up one of his friends in this job. He is only waiting for some reason or justification to act.'

M. le Chef stood up and began to walk about the room. This was an event rare in any interview and therefore significant of his mental agitation. M. Pinaud waited, outwardly calm, inwardly seething with indignation and frustration and disappointment and bitterness.

'So you see it is not easy. I have to be careful. I must be extremely careful. I am compelled by these facts to be more than careful. My enemies are ready—waiting for me to slip, to make just one mistake, which will give them the excuse they want to get rid of me. Therefore I have to interpret all instructions and directions literally, according to the exact meaning of the printed words—there is no longer any margin for my own decisions.'

'But this is a question of—' began M. Pinaud.

'I know, Pinaud—I know. I quite agree with you. You know and I know—after all that you have done over the past years for me and this department—that had it been possible I would have authorized the expense myself without hesitation. But now such a thing is completely out of the question. It is beyond my powers. It is no longer in my hands.'

He walked back to his chair and sat down. He did not look at M. Pinaud but eyed the sheet of paper in front of him morosely. Suddenly he snatched it up, tore it across viciously and flung the pieces in the wastepaper basket.

M. Pinaud took a deep breath.

'If you will pardon me m'sieu,' he said forcefully, 'and remember that I am speaking with all due respect, may I presume to point out that what you have just told me has been most interesting, completely surprising—and nothing at all to do with the point at issue.'

'What do you mean?'

'Either this your establishment functions efficiently or it does not function at all. This is not a question of economy or policy, but of plain commonsense. A schoolboy of fourteen could understand. Either I get a new car or else I go on in this one and one day I break my neck or a murderer escapes or both.'

M. le Chef looked at him curiously.

'I have seldom seen you so bitter, Pinaud,' he said quietly.

'Bitter?' M. Pinaud exploded. 'Of course I am bitter. This is a situation calculated to produce bitterness as easily and as naturally as a mother produces milk. When I see and hear all these new, young and brash detectives boasting of their up-to-date models and what performance they give on the road, while I have to keep my old car year after year—can you wonder I become bitter?

'Why not give a new model to me? There always seems to be enough money for new models for new detectives— why isn't there any for me? After all, I have worked for you now for some eighteen years, m'sieu, and—as you yourself have been kind and gracious enough to point out on various occasions—not entirely without some small success.

'Why not pass on my old car to one of these new boys? You must admit that what they achieve in the first two years of their employment—while they are growing up and making all the idiotic mistakes from which the intelligent ones will learn how to be efficient—could just as easily be performed in the front seat of an old car. One does not need the latest model to act like an idiot. But you know and I know, m'sieu, how many times my car and my driving has saved my life, captured a criminal and brought a certain amount of prestige and fame to this your department.'

He paused, more through lack of breath than paucity of ideas. M. le Chef answered him with commendable restraint.

'Believe me, Pinaud, I see your point of veiw. But it is not practical.'

M. Pinaud swiftly thought of an answer to that one. He could have retorted that his point of view was infinitely more practical than the attitude of sitting on one's backside trying to achieve the impossible by interpreting bureaucratic directives without making hypothetical mistakes—but this was not the time to be rude.

He needed a new car. And he—what with money to find to pay for gas bills and rent and food and new clothes for two growing girls—was hardly in a position to sign a cheque to pay for one. M. le Chef, with some little encouragement, was.

He opened his mouth with a view to providing this encouragement, but he was too late. M. le Chef was already speaking.

'You must appreciate, Pinaud, the difficulties we are having these days in getting the force recruited up to strength. With all the prevalent violence and sadism which has become an inherent part of organized crime and the consequent and ever-increasing dangers in our profession, it is getting harder and harder to attract the right type of man. It is not only economically essential—in view of the salary scale laid down at the beginning of the century by the establishment—but psychologically sound to offer each recruit a new car as an inducement to joining the force. We need these young men, Pinaud—it is a young man's world today.'

M. le Chef paused for a moment and sighed.

'Let us face it, Pinaud,' he continued quietly and perhaps a little sadly, 'you and I are not getting any younger. We must have this new and young blood—we need its energy and its new and forceful ideas like a transfusion.'

M. Pinaud looked at him coldly. When his own employer began talking cock, there was little an employee could do. He would have liked a cigarette, but then no one ever smoked in the presence of M. le Chef.

'You may be speaking for yourself, m'sieu,' he said slowly, choosing his words with great care, 'as you are fully entitled to, but you are certainly not speaking for me. I may not be getting any younger, but I do not feel old. I may be getting old but I do not feel old. That is a state of mind. Mercifully, I have not got it. And I certainly do not agree with you that it is a young man's world today. Except insofar as—in spite of the Pill—it seems to be full of them and they all think they know everything. Experience and intelligence are so much more important, but these take years to acquire. Their new cars and their energy and their young blood will not stop them having their heads blown off when they drive up in a hurry in front of a criminal with a gun. Those who survive will learn the hard way, as we all had to do.'

He paused only long enough to take a deep breath.

'However, all this is academic and perhaps has little to do with my request for a new car. I only mentioned it in the hope that it might have helped you to understand something of my bitterness. I feel that I am being most unfairly and most unjustly treated. This is not what I had expected—as I am sure you will understand—as a recompense for years of loyal and faithful service to the department. When I consider—'

M. le Chef sighed. It was not a particularly loud sigh, and yet clearly audible, as it was meant to be, and it effectively put an end to whatever M. Pinaud had been about to consider.

'I told you, Pinaud,' he interrupted, with the faintest and yet unmistakable traces of exasperation underlying his tone, 'I told you that I fully agree with you and have every sympathy for your feelings, which under the circumstances are quite natural and entirely justified. I also told you and tried to make you understand—and obviously have completely failed—that these circumstances are exceptional and entirely and absolutely beyond my control. We shall just have to leave it at that.'

He stood up and did not walk about the room, which meant that the interview was over.

M. Pinaud sighed too. He sighed for all the frustration and the disappointment and the despair and the disillusion inherent in being born a perfectionist—but unlike M. le Chef, his sigh was inaudible. Years of experience and practice had conditioned him to keep his features impassive, masking his outraged and turbulent feelings.

'Very well, m'sieu. Thank you for granting me this interview. I am sorry it has resulted in nothing and I hope I have not wasted too much of your valuable time.'

He walked towards the door. With his hand on the latch he turned, and in spite of himself his voice quivered with an emotion he could not control.

'But I leave you, m'sieu, filled with the most gloomy and despairing forebodings. This car of mine has already done all that could reasonably be expected of it. Indeed, it has done more. That is why I talk to it. If gratitude is felt, one should express it, either in words or actions.'

He opened the door wide, stepped over the threshold and then turned around again. Before he closed it he spoke once more.

'But mark my words, m'sieu—no one and no piece of machinery can do the impossible. One day, sooner or later, that car is bound to let me down. I shall not blame it. I shall speak no word of recrimination or reproach. I shall not lose my temper. I shall not kick it, mouthing filthy abuse, as I have seen young and impatient drivers doing.

'Mind you, I may not be able to speak at all, because I

shall probably be dead and some murderer will be driving away from the wreck down the same road, laughing all over his evil and ugly face.'

'You always look on the black side of things, Pinaud,' M. le Chef retorted calmly, from the exact centre of that magnificent Aubusson carpet. 'And I have noticed of late a definite tendency you seem to have acquired to exaggerate, quite deliberately, in order to achieve an effect—the effect you desire. The result of indulging in this poetic licence is certainly melodramatic, but not always strictly accurate.'

'I am not exaggerating, m'sieu,' replied M. Pinaud gravely. 'Obviously I am pointing out the most extreme results of this policy you seem determined to pursue. There are others—not so serious, but which might well cause untold harm. I could be late for an important appointment. I could promise—in all good faith—to be somewhere and end up somewhere else. In a garage behind a breakdown van. And in the end arrive later—much later. The consequences for the person waiting might be serious—have you considered that aspect of the matter?'

His words were bitter, filled with righteous indignation and quivering with emotion. He could not know that they were also prophetic.

M. le Chef sat down in his chair, opened a drawer on the side of his desk and extracted a new and single sheet of paper. He placed this carefully in the exact centre of his blotting-pad. His voice was tired and without emotion.

'I have considered every aspect of the matter, Pinaud. I can only repeat that my hands are tied, and hope that you will believe me. I can do nothing about it.'

'Very well, m'sieu.'

M. Pinaud shut the door. He felt like banging it, but he closed it quietly.

There was a café near the office building which most of the detectives frequented in their spare time.

M. Pinaud felt like a drink before going home. A small flat—which was all he could afford on his pitiful salary—

occupied by a wife and two growing girls, was hardly an ideal place in which to drink, when there was so much to forget.

Sometimes—after a particularly nerve-racking and difficult case—he felt unable to resist the compulsion and would quickly dispose of half a bottle of absinthe before his dinner, if only to deaden the agony some of his day's work had caused him.

Germaine never made any comment. But he sensed and felt her disapproval, her pity and her concern as deeply as if she had shouted and screamed at him—even louder, because he knew that it was only her love and her anxiety for him and his health that prompted it, and therefore—silent and unspoken and unexpressed—it lay like a constraint between them and got on his nerves and eventually tasted stronger even than the absinthe . . .

No—this was a time when the drink was needed, quickly and silently and efficiently, without talk, without disapproval, without unspoken comment or unexpressed condemnation—if only to wash the taste of this monstrous injustice from his throat and eradicate its bitterness from his still seething and fermenting mind.

Two of the young new detectives were seated at a table and looked up as he came in.

'Hullo there, M'sieu Pinaud,' called one of them cheerfully. 'Come and join us for a drink.'

He hesitated. The last thing he wanted to do just then was to drink and talk. His only ambition was to drink— and drink again—and thereby perhaps achieve the difficult task of not thinking. And yet it would be churlish to refuse, rude and ill-mannered to decline the invitation, extended so obviously in goodwill and sincerity.

The hesitation only lasted for a second. He smiled, and the brooding harshness of his features was transfigured.

'How kind of you. I probably look as though I needed one.'

The other young man pulled out a chair and the waiter appeared quickly.

'Pernod, if you please,' said M. Pinaud. 'Let me see—I

know you both by sight. You have been here some weeks now, I believe. But you must forgive me—I do not know your names—'

The first young man, the one who had called out, had a charming smile.

'I am Robert Dupuis, and this is Yves Lorraine,' he said. 'No one ever expected you to remember them after we were introduced. But we had no difficulty—had we, Yves? —in remembering yours, M'sieu Pinaud.'

They both laughed easily. He found their gaiety, their good spirits and their cheerfulness quite fascinating.

'Why not?' he asked.

'After all the things the old fool told us in his speech about you,' said Yves, 'it would have been like forgetting the catechism or your mother's Christian name.'

They both roared with laughter, completely oblivious of the others in the café. M. Pinaud noticed that the enormous two-litre bottle of wine in front of them was nearly empty. Perhaps the salary scales of the department had been brought up-to-date and M. le Chef had omitted to tell him.

When the waiter brought his absinthe, he felt in his pocket, but Robert laid a hand quickly on his arm.

'Please—we invited you,' he said.

'In that case I am grateful,' M. Pinaud replied courteously, but went on feeling in his pocket until he found a note. 'But nevertheless allow me—in view of your most charming compliment—to make this one small gesture.'

He gave the note to the waiter.

'Another bottle, please, for these two gentlemen.'

They both thanked him, politely and sincerely. He looked at them with renewed interest. They were both young. Both wore their hair longer than he would ever have permitted his own to grow. Their suits were sharp and fashionable, their shirts and ties vividly bright and—to his old-fashioned taste—even violent.

Robert had a moustache which reminded M. Pinaud of an engraving he had once seen of Genghis Khan. Yves was clean-shaven, with two rows of impeccable false teeth shining whitely whenever he smiled. They both exuded a vitality, a confidence and an optimism which made him, un-accountably, feel suddenly very old.

He had hardly finished his absinthe when the waiter, in response to Yves' lordly gesture, brought him another one.

'I was telling Robert here,' said Yves, dismissing his attempt at thanks with a wave of his hand, 'just when you came in, M'sieu Pinaud—what a good job it is they have given us a decent car—'

'We could never do the job without one,' put in Robert, pouring out the new bottle of wine with all the uninhibited delight of a child who has found an unexpected treasure in his Christmas stocking.

'You can say that again,' replied Yves, swallowing the contents of his glass and pushing it forward across the table in almost the same movement. 'You could never even begin to do a job like this in an old banger. Yesterday I was chasing the forger Marquand. I was trying to catch him all the way from the Gare St Lazare to Thiers. He had a Citroën—a good one—but he never had the nerve to let it out, or else he would have lost me easily. I held him on the hills and the corners. I was doing over a hundred in third gear for the last hour.'

'No overheating?' asked Robert.

'Not a sign. Needle steady as a rock.'

'I know. They are marvellous cars,' said Robert, grasping the bottle and pouring with an enthusiasm that almost compensated for his wavering hand. 'I had to go to the coast last week in a hurry. We got a telephone-call from a stoolie at Dieppe about some smugglers' meeting and they thought it would be a good idea if I attended as a free-lance fisherman. By the time I had found some clothes there was hardly and time left to get there. I had to go like the clappers—foot flat down on the pedal or flat down on the brake—one, two, one, two—all the way.'

He laughed cheerfully and drained his glass.

'But what a car. What magnificent brakes. You would never know you were on the road—a wet one or a greasy one. When you stick them on it's like pulling up in a train, with all the wheels held between two rails.'

M. Pinaud looked at them with interest and admiration.

With one swallow he finished his absinthe. These were the new *élite*, the rulers of the world, the givers of the blood-transfusion so necessary for those of his generation.

As he looked from them both back to his empty glass, he saw that the waiter was busily engaged in refilling it.

Perhaps it was just as well, he thought sombrely, because intermingled now with all his interest and all his admiration, he knew there was a touch of sadness, and a note of bitterness, which a drink—especially a dangerous drink like absinthe—would certainly help to alleviate and mitigate, softening and soothing the sharp edges of pain.

'Tell me,' he said gravely, 'what happened when you got to the meeting at Dieppe?'

For one fleeting second Robert seemed to lose a fraction of his aplomb. He clutched the bottle and poured drinks almost feverishly, as if in self-vindication.

'I never got there,' he said. 'Some bastard in a tractor came out of a field and bashed me up.'

'That was hard luck,' M. Pinaud replied, his voice expressionless.

When he had cause to apply his brakes in an emergency, particularly on a wet or greasy road, his own car usually shot off at a tangent of forty-five degrees. He had never been fortunate enough to enjoy the privileges of a train-driver who could stop in a hurry with the confidence of knowing that all his wheels were firmly aligned between two railway lines. Even so, in a lifetime of driving, often under appalling weather conditions and sometimes with his life literally depending on the speed of his car, he had never failed to see and to avoid a tractor—even driven by a bastard—coming out of a field.

'But there was not much damage, anyway,' broke in the irrepressible Robert, drinking heartily in sheer thankfulness at the comforting thought. 'A new front assembly—lights—bumpers—bonnet-catch—radiator and wings—that's all. They did it in two days.'

'All covered by the insurance,' put in Yves, his teeth seeming to gleam and shine in benediction both of their loss and his comrade's gain.

'And you,' said M. Pinaud, turning to him with equal

gravity. 'What happened about Marquand—did you catch him?'

'No, M'sieu Pinaud.'

In spite of the negative answer, all the teeth glittered at him happily and confidently.

'There was an awful lot of traffic in the centre of the town and I was compelled to lie quite a few cars back. I finally caught up with the Citroën, forced him to stop and prepared to do my stuff—you know—jingling the old handcuffs and brandishing the old cannon—and then I saw that there was some other character at the wheel, wearing the same coat and hat. They must have done the switch in the traffic.'

And they both roared again with laughter, as if at the greatest joke in the world. Then they concentrated on finishing the bottle of wine, as if that were of far greater importance than the mere failure of a mission.

M. Pinaud sat there quietly, smiling politely, if abstractedly, at their jokes.

Sometimes, with this new generation, he had the feeling that he was living in another world, so alien and incomprehensible was theirs to him.

To allow the forger to get away with the oldest trick in the world—to let him infiltrate into the heart of the traffic before making the arrest was bad enough—but to laugh like an idiot at his own failure—that was something he would never understand.

No sign of remorse, he noticed—no determination to profit from the experience—no admittance or acknowledgment of any mistake or miscalculation—no pride in his work—no conscientiousness—no sense of responsibility or devotion to duty—only that sheer happy light-heartedness and insouciance . . .

It was all very strange and disturbing. And somehow filled with bitterness.

And for this they both got paid—enough to afford two-litre bottles of wine—and supplied with new cars.

He finished his drink, thanked them both politely and wished them well, refused their offer of another one and went home.

2

But the bitterness stayed within him, a quiet and insidious poison that flowed with and through his blood at the pumping of his heart, that therefore permeated and polluted his whole being, that made him irritable when he got home, silent and morose while he ate his dinner, thoughtless and even unknowingly cruel as he refused a sweet his wife had spent hours in making, and cold and remote and withdrawn and abstracted as he sat in the old and comfortable armchair afterwards in front of the gas-fire.

Normally, he ate with a vast and voracious appetite. Usually, as soon as he arrived home, he shed all the cares and the anxieties and the frustrations and even the terrors of the day like an old and friendly and shabby coat, easily and quickly and effortlessly, and praised his wife's cooking and kept his daughters in fits of laughter as he described and altered and modified and embellished the stark and gruesome tragedies which often had comprised his day.

Now he sat alone, absorbed in a world of his own.

One daughter brought in his tray of coffee, the other the bottle of kirsch and a small glass.

He thanked them politely, not seeing them. They fled back to the kitchen and the washing-up—to the security of familiar things and the warmth and the comfort and the sheer accessibility of their mother's love.

M. Pinaud brooded in front of the gas-fire—a cheap and cheerful fire—his thoughts blackened and corroded and polluted with bitterness.

For eighteen years he had captured criminals and solved insoluble mysteries and risked his life and his health for the triumph of justice and the honour and glory of M. le Chef. So—it could hardly be deemed a reward and therefore should be considered as a result—so he sat in front of a gas-fire—a very cheap and not particularly cheerful gas-fire—with its bloody insipid jets flaring and popping spasmodically and reminding him continuously how the

bills grew greater every quarter—while M. le Chef lolled
at ease in a fifteenth-century wing-chair before a blazing
log-fire in the huge stone fireplace of his mediaeval manor-
house. This day being Friday, he would have left the office
an hour early to drive home to his country house in
Pontlieu.

M. Pinaud drank his coffee, which was deliciously strong
and scalding hot, and sipped his kirsch, which had been
distilled illicitly for him as a token of appreciation and
gratitude by a farmer in Switzerland and which must have
been from its taste at least ninety-nine per cent proof—and
allowed his vivid imagination free rein.

Should he write a letter of resignation?

This is to confirm in writing, four weeks in advance as
per the terms of my contract, that I wish to terminate my
employment with the Department of the *Sûreté* in Paris.
I have neither the inclination nor the obligation—as the
fifty-eight clauses of the contract will confirm—to accept
the treatment of a pig as a reward for eighteen years of
loyal and faithful service.

There—that would make them think. That would get
them off their backsides, embedded for so many years in
comfortable chairs. Some might even stand up. Perhaps
these new and omnipotent young detectives, with their
blood-transfusions clutched in their hands, might even get,
as a result of his letter, not only new cars regularly, but
new and fairer contracts as well.

But then if he resigned, what job could he do? How
could he earn enough money to support a family?

Most firms would regret politely and show him the door
—this was a young man's world, as M. le Chef had pointed
out. He did not feel old, but he probably looked old. The
strains and stresses of a lifetime's dangerous living had
obviously left their ineradicable imprint on his features.

What could he do? What qualifications could he offer,
after a lifetime spent in catching criminals?

His depression and his bitterness inevitably led his
thoughts away from those very assets which had made the
success of his career possible, and plunged him even deeper
into the slough of introspection.

I could become a criminal myself, he reflected moodily. And probably a successful one. There is no mystery, no secret about the profession—no years of apprenticeship and training required, no examinations to pass. All one needs is a logical mind, and the ability to plan carefully and methodically and meticulously, and to make allowances and counter-plans in advance for every eventuality and contingency, for every unforeseen development, for every unexpected emergency which can always nullify the most brilliant plan . . .

His thoughts ran on and on. Then the door opened and his wife came in to take his coffee-tray and the girls to say good night—and he came back to earth and realised that a man with the privileges and the responsibilities of such a wonderful family had no business to contemplate crime as a career.

Shortly before midnight the telephone rang in the hall.

He was still awake. At once he began to get out of the bed, carefully and slowly, so as not to disturb his wife. He need not have troubled—after the way and the hours Germaine worked every day, she had no difficulty in sleeping the sleep of the exhausted—but it was typical of his nature and his consideration for other people that he took infinite care and pains over the operation.

At length, after opening and closing the two doors quietly, he lifted the receiver and ended that insistent and monotonous ringing.

'Yes,' he said quietly. 'Pinaud here.'

M. le Chef's voice, he had come to realize over a considerable period of time, had as many inflections as the years themselves, but now this was one he did not recognize.

'Thank God you heard the bell—I apologize for disturbing you—'

'I was not asleep, m'sieu.'

'Good. Listen, Pinaud—I am in trouble—terrible trouble. Can you come out here to Pontlieu tonight—at once—now?'

This was not M. le Chef the autocrat, the supreme commander, the individualist, the arbiter of destinies and sal-aries—this was a man upset and desperate and even afraid.

'Well,' replied M. Pinaud slowly and carefully, 'I sup-pose I could, if it is really necessary. It is only about an hour's run. But what is the trouble, m'sieu? What has happened?'

'I am alone in the house—my wife is away. My new housemaid is dead in my bed. She had been murdered—a violent blow on the head with some heavy instrument. I went out for a short while. When I came back I found her there like that.'

There was a silence after he had spoken which M. Pinaud found unendurable. He broke it by speaking quickly and decisively, deliberately making no comment on what he had just heard.

'I see. Very well, m'sieu. I will be there in about an hour. Goodbye for now.'

He opened the bedroom door quietly, scooped up an armful of his clothes, took clean shirts and underclothes from his wardrobe, and went back into the hall, closing the door behind him.

He dressed quickly, found his valise in the hall cup-board, packed it methodically with what he would need and then wrote a note to his wife explaining what had happened.

Once again he tiptoed into the bedroom and laid it on his pillow. He stood there for a moment, irresolute, his hand still outstretched. He would have liked to kiss her goodbye. He never knew, when he left in this manner, whether he would ever return. A man who could batter a young girl to death in bed would have little compunction in killing an interfering detective who tried to arrest him.

On the other hand, his commonsense reassured him, he had crept out in this way countless times before, and always the good God had protected him and kept him unharmed in His holy care and sent him back home safely to the wife and the children he loved so much.

Most of the troubles in his life had never happened. It was more important—in view of all the work that would confront her the next day—that his wife should enjoy a good night's rest, without worrying about him and his participation in the complications which a schoolboy could have foreseen would inevitably result from a sex-life as involved as that of M. le Chef . . .

His car started at the first touch of the key. He lit a cigarette and sat there meditating for a moment, letting the engine run quietly and smoothly, as was his habit before driving off.

This was not an appeal he could ignore. Not even his bitterness could stifle the instantaneous response which to one of his nature was instinctive. A man was in trouble. If everyone helped, he would get out of it. Those better qualified to help could do more. The end result would be the more quickly achieved. This was the whole point and meaning of friendship.

There were certain people in the world today, he knew, whose attitude towards their fellow-men and philosophy of life was admirably condensed and expressed by the immortal Army slogan—pull up the tail-board, chum, I'm on board—but mercifully he was not one of them.

He was old-fashioned—granted. He had been brought up—mercifully—in an old-fashioned and strict way, for which he never ceased to be truly thankful. He was one of those who needed a blood-transfusion from this breed of aggressive youth who would shortly inherit and rule the earth—that could be.

But over the years in the past—those years which had succeeded each other with such a remorseless finality and which had differed so inexplicably and so tragically each one from the other—the bonds of friendship and understanding had been forged, strongly and enduringly, between him and his employer, with each terrible and macabre experience succeeding each other like another hammer blow to fuse the white-hot metal—with the greying and cooling flakes that seemed part of M. le Chef's difficult and sometimes impossible character flying off, each time a little more, from the anvil to the packed and beaten and earthen floor . . .

And these bonds had been so well forged they were now too strong to break.

He sighed, put the car in gear, let in his clutch and drove away to Pontlieu.

It should take him about an hour, he thought. Since the road would be deserted at this hour, he could drive really fast and cut down the time, bearing in mind the anxiety and the desperation he had heard in M. le Chef's voice.

He pressed the accelerator and the car roared on through the city, out under the Porte de Saint Ouen and along the lonely and sleeping Route Nationale.

Always when he drove, whatever his speed, he found time to glance at the instruments on his dashboard. This, he would undoubtedly have pointed out to M. le Chef, had the expression on that worthy's face in the morning been one of sympathy, was one of the vital links of communication between them. How else could he tell—since the car, whatever its almost human capabilities, was unable to speak—how else could he tell that every component in that beautiful engine was working and functioning as it should?

Now he looked—quickly, automatically and yet carefully as was his habit—and was horrified to see that his heat-gauge was rising rapidly. The hand was almost on the red danger division of the dial.

He slowed down instinctively and concentrated his gaze no longer on the dashboard but on the various landmarks outside to determine exactly where he was. He knew the road well and soon realized thankfully that he was not far from Villars, which was a fairly large town which should have an all-night garage.

He always checked his radiator and oil-level so often and so conscientiously that he knew with a positive conviction that the cause did not lie there. Something was broken. Something had worn out and broken.

Yet—although one might have thought it inevitable—this conclusion, logical and ultimately proved correct, did not lead him to think at all about M. le Chef and his interview that morning. He was far too busy, driving slowly and carefully, and glancing anxiously and alternately at the heat-indicator and out at the road ahead and wondering whether he would get to Villars before the engine boiled.

He would not have been human had he not remembered the cheerful words of Yves that evening—needle steady as a rock as he roared up the savage corners of the Central Massif in third gear—but resolutely he put both them and their bitterness out of his mind.

There were more important things to be done now. He could allow memory to come another time. If his vivid imagination saw the teeth, shining and gleaming happily in the windscreen, he could ignore them and look beyond them—they might encourage him, but they would not help him to get to Villars.

'Inlet hose,' bawled the garage-man cheerfully and yet at the same time accusingly and menacingly, whipping open the bonnet with one powerful hand and waving a spanner at M. Pinaud's head with the other. 'Bound to be inlet hose, from what you tell me. If it had been inlet, you would have had no water left by now. Where did you say you came from—the city?'

'Yes, I—'

'Start the engine, m'sieu, if you please.'

'But—'

'Start the engine, I said. How else can I see the water?'

Obediently M. Pinaud started his beloved engine, with trepidation and misgiving. Surely this could not possibly do it any good, at that temperature and with so little water left in the radiator.

But with all the garages listed in the *Département de l'Oise,* he seemed to have picked the operating centre of a fanatic. The only consolation was that this individual, short and burly, rude and aggressive and self-opinionated and ill-mannered, did at least appear to know his job.

'There—what did I tell you?' bawled the garage-man in a veritable paxroysm of triumph and delight, pointing to the thin jets of steam and drops of water hissing and bubbling from the rubber connection. 'All right—switch off.'

M. Pinaud switched off.

'Rubber is perishable,' he was told sternly. 'Didn't you even think of checking those connections?'

'I did—often. They looked all right to me.'

'Ah—but it is on the underneath they perish—on the inside of the bend.'

'I did not know that,' said M. Pinaud meekly. Although he knew a little about an astonishing number of things, the longer he lived the more he realized, with commendable humility, the extent of his ignorance. 'I do not usually run such an old car—'

'Old?' the man interrupted fiercely. 'This engine is not old. It is in beautiful condition. It will still be running when you and I are dead, m'sieu.'

In view of his recent telephone conversation, this was hardly a subject on which M. Pinaud cared to dwell, and therefore he made no comment. This man obviously knew his job. He might even be psychic as well.

Astonishingly, the bonnet was not slammed down but lowered carefully and even reverently.

'I must congratulate you, m'sieu, on the condition of your engine,' the man said in a very civil voice, entirely different from his previous aggressive and hectoring tone. 'And its exceptional cleanliness. It will be a pleasure to work on it.'

'Thank you,' replied M. Pinaud, with equal courtesy. 'How long do you think—'

'About an hour. Less than that, possibly, although I must check the outlet hose as well. I will do it right away.'

'Good. Is there a café open near, where I could have some coffee?'

'Yes. Turn right—a few doors down.'

'Thank you.'

'You are welcome.'

Madame in the café was still young, but looked old. Her eyes were large and brown and once had been beautiful. Now they were bleak and hard and cold. Her body sagged, broken with child-bearing and hard work.

She looked at him without interest and eyed his money as though it might be false. He was just another man. The world had obviously been harsh and cruel to her, largely because of the men who inhabited it. One more coming into her café to buy coffee could not make any difference to anything now and therefore was not important. The profit on coffee would not pay the bills.

M. Pinaud consumed a whole pot of black coffee, because by now he was beginning to feel sleepy.

He looked at the telephone on the wall several times while he was drinking and smoking, thought about it, pondered the thought, and then finally decided against making a call to explain the delay.

In his present state of tension and emotion, M. le Chef would probably have a heart-attack as soon as the bell rang in that silent house, whose only other occupant was a dead girl in his bed.

Far better to let him wait an extra half-hour. He might even recall, while waiting, their conversation that morning. He would realize, once again, that Pinaud was usually right, even though no one in the Department ever seemed to take any notice of him, or even listen or do anything about his complaints. In any case, whatever he thought would be preferable to dropping dead on the stone floor.

He glanced at his watch. Forty-five minutes had elapsed. It was time he went to see how the repairs were progressing. He could always drive a little faster, to make up some of the time lost.

He found his car with the bonnet still up, two powerful inspection lamps rigged underneath, and what looked like most of his engine in pieces on the cement floor, which mercifully seemed to be immaculately clean. Two overall-clad figures were working busily and silently side by side.

As he came in, one of them straightened at the sound of his footsteps and turned to meet him. It was the garage-man, sweating and oily, but still triumphant.

'I checked the outlet, m'sieu, after I had replaced the inlet. That was all right. Then I started the engine to check. The water still came out. Your main gasket has gone as well. I assumed you wanted to get on, so I got some help. I hope I did right. This is a big job, even for two.'

M. Pinaud looked at him in dismay. Then he took out his packet of cigarettes and automatically proffered it. The man shook his head.

'Not now, thank you, m'sieu.'

'Of course. I am sorry—I was thinking about the delay. You were quite right to get on with it—and I am very grateful. How long—'

'Three or four hours more, I am afraid—even with the two of us.'

'Is there any hope of hiring a car? I have a very important appointment in Pontlieu.'

The garage-man looked at something beneath a coat of grease and oil on his wrist that might have been a watch and shook his head decisively.

'Not at this time, m'sieu. It is nearly one o'clock. We are the only garage that keeps open all night and we do not keep cars for hire. It would not pay us. There is a late taxi service in the town, but he shuts at midnight.'

'Trains?'

'Nothing now. We are not on the main line here.'

'Any chance of a lift?'

He felt he had to try everything to get there. The voice he could still hear in his mind was as clear and as desperate as it had been on the telephone.

The man shook his head.

'This is a main road. There is always some traffic, and of course the all-night lorries. But very few stop nowadays—you realize that, don't you? There have been too many incidents, especially at night.'

'I know.'

'And then, if I remember, Pontlieu is a good way to the west, isn't it?'

'Yes. You take the fork at Lasagne.'

'Then that is where you would be dropped—at the fork. And have to walk what—ten, fifteen kilometres?'

'At least.'

M. Pinaud sighed despondently. The garage-man turned back to the car.

'I would not waste time even thinking about it, m'sieu,' he said cheerfully. 'You go and have some more of that excellent coffee. And ask Madame for some of her special *cognac* if you are feeling cold—and we will get you to Pontlieu as soon as anybody.'

If his hands had not been covered in oil and grease, M. Pinaud had the feeling that he would have slapped this unexpected and thrice-welcome client heartily on the back, by way of encouragement.

It was all right for him, thought M. Pinaud a little bit-terly—he is only triumphant and cheerful because he is adding up in his mind all the time he is working how much he is going to charge me for the repair.

But then, almost as soon as it came, he dismissed the thought, not without a certain shame, as unworthy and unjust. The man was right and his advice had been good.

So he thanked him politely and made his way back to the café.

The brandy was excellent and remarkably cheap. He did not see any bottle. Madame brought it to his table, pre-sumably drawn from a cask, in a large tumbler.

Moodily he drank it and ordered another pot of black coffee. When that came, he held out the glass and asked for another. For a second a flash of some indefinable emotion seemed to bring life into the bleak cold eyes.

Although the brandy was both cheap and excellent, he thought, perhaps there was more profit on it than on coffee.

She brought the glass back to his table for the second time, took his money and then stood there beside him, wrapping her faded and not too clean dressing-gown closer about her.

'M'sieu is a traveller?' she asked.

'No.'

He did not feel like talking.

'M'sieu has car trouble—at the all-night garage?' she persisted.

'Yes.'

'I thought so. All clients at this time have car trouble.'

He looked at her with pity and compassion. Life had not been easy for this one. He made a great effort to be polite.

'Then they are fortunate indeed, to find you here open

at this hour, Madame, with your most excellent coffee and *cognac.*'

'I have to keep open,' she replied dully, 'to make the place pay.'

He picked up the glass and drank some of the brandy. He felt that he ought to offer her something, but he was not in the mood for polite conversation. He wondered if she had a husband who would open the café in the morning, so that she could get some sleep. From the look of her it did not seem likely.

'It is cold outside,' she said.

'Yes.'

'The coffee—it is warming.'

'Yes.'

'The *cognac* is even more warming.'

'Yes.'

He wondered where this conversation was leading. He was not left in doubt for long.

'Would M'sieu perhaps fancy something a little more warming—something better than coffee or *cognac?*'

In spite of himself he looked at her incredulously. For one terrible and agonizing second a great bitterness flooded and melted the brown eyes and he cursed himself for his thoughtlessness in causing her pain.

'Oh—not myself, m'sieu. It is years since a man looked at me with lust. But upstairs I have a daughter—'

'No—' exploded M. Pinaud violently.

Now the brown eyes were once again bleak and cold and hard.

'A lovely young daughter, m'sieu. She is still at school—but her body has to be seen to be believed. She will come down if I tell her.'

'Are you seriously suggesting—'

'Of course I am,' she interrupted him calmly. 'And she is still a virgin.'

'Do you think that I—'

'Of course I do. You are a man. All men are the same. There is only one thing men want in this life.'

'I am sorry but—'

'They try to disguise it and put elegant names on it—

but anyone with any sense always knows. They insist on marrying a virgin and after two or three children come they lose interest. Why? They married a virgin. Where is she now?'

'I have no desire to—'

'Some men are different,' she interrupted him again, studying him critically and appraisingly. 'This is how we are born. We cannot change what we inherit. My daughter has a brother. He is beautiful. He will do what I tell him to do. Would you—'

'Madame,' M. Pinaud interrupted in his turn, very firmly. 'You are wasting your time. I am going to sit here, drinking your coffee and your *cognac*, until my car is ready. That is all. Then I am leaving.'

'But—'

'You heard what I said. That is enough.'

She recognized the finality in his tone, shrugged and walked back to the bar.

M. Pinaud lit a fresh cigarette, more shaken than he would have believed possible. He would have to get Pujol, his old friend from the vice-squad, to call on her as soon as he could. He felt glad he did not have Pujol's job.

He tried to shut it all from his mind, but it was not easy. With an effort of will, he forced himself to consider his present situation.

He took out his pocket-book, turned his back to the bar, and began to count the few notes he always kept in the reserve compartment. Over the past few months, these irritating and infuriating breakdowns had occurred with ever-increasing frequency, hence his not unreasonable request that morning. No—not that morning, he thought morosely and bitterly. It was late or early enough now to recall it as yesterday morning.

He had therefore been compelled for some time now to carry with him a considerable amount of money, in order to get himself out of trouble and keep on the road. He always added these amounts with the receipts to his expense-account and was duly reimbursed, but the margin between his income and his expenditure was narrow enough to make this on occasions most inconvenient.

With this money, he reflected gloomily, had M. le Chef been reasonable, he could have bought a new suit, or new shoes for his daughters. And the old idiot had never seen him so bitter—it was hardly surprising.

That train of thought sent him to the telephone.

The bell rang continuously, but there was no answer. He remembered, from past occasions, that there was an extension beside the bed. Its present occupant could hardly be expected to answer, but one would have thought that somewhere in the house another instrument had been installed.

Perhaps M. le Chef had given up expecting him and finally gone to sleep in another bedroom from which he could not hear the bell.

He went back to his table. He would try again later. In the intervals he could keep on drinking coffee and brandy —provided Madame continued to serve him—and smoke more than was good for him. And then he could always count his money again and try to calculate what the bill for the repair would be.

The hours would pass, as they always did—not happily, not joyfully, not ecstatically. But they would pass.

3

Golden in the radiance of his headlights, the road raced
to meet him. The powerful beam cut a swathe of light
through the blackness of the grass on either side of its endless symmetry. The massive trunks of the poplar trees fled
by as if on fire, the arms of their branches spreading closely
above him to enclose and contain that tunnel of light, the
hands and fingers of their leaves invisible in the darkness
about its reach.

He felt alone, speeding behind and through a world that
did not exist, at the trail of a comet of light that was
hurtling through the black vastness of the unknown.

On and on he drove, through sleeping villages and
shuttered houses, past lonely and isolated farms, between
endless fields and orchards and forests, until gradually, im-
perceptibly, the darkness melted into grey and the grey
grew paler and lighter with the first faint flushing of an
unseen sun, the trees grew blacker by contrast, the glow
from his lights less intense and the unknown world on
either side now a vastness that had depth and meaning as
he roared on to meet the dawn.

He came to Pontlieu and the old manor-house in the
early morning, with the singing of the birds filling the air
with an ecstatic and quivering chorus of sound.

The massive iron-studded door, recessed in a stone arch
that would not have disgraced a cathedral, was shut.

He parked his car neatly in the drive beside a glittering
red Ferrari drop-head coupé. He had heard of this car
from M. le Chef. It belonged to his wife.

He got out and walked over to look at it with interest.
The top was down, and from the dew on the upholstery
the car had been left open all night. The key was in the
ignition-switch. On the carpet, almost hidden by the over-
hang of the passenger-seat, was a massive tyre-lever.

Wondering, he walked back to the house.

Parts of the lower walls looked as though their stones

had been laid in the time when the country grew from that island in the Seine which the Vikings once burnt. The remainder of the manor-house had probably been built on these foundations at a later date.

For a moment he stood there, his hand outstretched, while his imagination, inspired by the beauty and the age of the building in front of him, raced with an almost feverish intensity.

These rough-hewn stones had heard prayers for the Crusades, had seen their Seigneur and his vassals ride off for Jerusalem—and centuries later, the farmwain creaking down the dusty road to the cobbles of Paris and the guillotine. They had heard violins playing from the minstrels' gallery inside the banqueting-hall—and listened to the screams of the peasants whom the men-at-arms flogged for not paying the salt-tax. They had seen spearmen and axemen and pikemen, priests and monks, pilgrims and Cardinals, warriors and clerks, wainwrights and armourers, jugglers and tumblers, stone-masons and carpenters—they had seen men kill each other in the cold grey light of dawn for an academic point of honour.

On the Eve of St Bartholomew one of the family had perhaps died with his back to that wall, parrying for mad and glorious moments the swords that flickered and darted before the white armlets of shame.

These same stones had watched the fair-haired Saxons marching, flushed with the triumph of Sedan. and in a new generation, the Renault taxis filled with cheering soldiers had swayed and lurched along that nearby road on their way to the Marne.

Somehow—inexplicably and yet with a strange and logical inevitability—these stones reminded him of the time when he had once knelt for his confirmation prayer in the carved richness of the church in his boyhood village.

And in the midst of all his thoughts, vivid and poignant, the memory of that prayer seemed to surge strongly, surely and sweetly to comfort him.

When he had finished that prayer and raised his head, the sun behind the one great circular window made the stained glass glow with exquisite colour. In one segment of traceried stone the blue shone with the brightness of the sky; beside it the red flamed like a setting autumnal sun. The purple and the gold glowed richly and passionately, as if eager to escape from the prison of glass, to which patient hands had borne the bright pigments, and limned them and fired them, confidently and lovingly, so many years ago . . .

Then he roused himself, pulled the handle of the bell-chain and listened to the deep and muted chimes of the bell through the old weathered planks. At the first note all the birds fell silent and he waited in a stillness that was absolute and strange in its intensity.

No one came. He waited and rang again. He tried the latch and pushed against the wood. From the feel of it the door was not only locked but bolted as well.

Not having brought with him either a battering-ram or high explosive, he turned away. Perhaps there was a back door, or an open window somewhere.

As he turned, he heard the click of the lock and the sound of bolts being withdrawn. The door opened. Balanced to a fine precision on its massive hinges, it swung easily and smoothly and silently.

M. Pinaud bowed politely. Many years ago, when he had been young and proud and ambitious, he had met M. le Chef's first wife. This one he had heard of but never met.

She was young—hardly more than a girl—and very lovely. Her body was small, but exquisitely proportioned. She had obviously been taking a shower. Her head was covered with a waterproof cap, on which the drops still glistened. The absence of any visible hair gave her features a childish and defenceless look that was strangely and disturbingly appealing. She wore a loose terrycloth robe and obviously nothing underneath. Where the robe did not meet, her skin was still wet.

M. Pinaud looked at her with a great intensity and forgot his fatigue and his sleepless night. Suddenly, almost desperately, he wanted to touch that wet skin and dry it, very gently and very tenderly and very carefully . . .

'Pinaud, from the *Sûreté*,' he began. 'Madame—'

'No,' she interrupted quickly. 'Not Madame—Lorette. I

have heard so much about you I feel I already know you well. Charles told me you were coming. But he expected you last night.'

'I know. I had car trouble.'

Then he made a great effort and looked from her body to her eyes. They were large and their colour was the vivid blue of gentians, and in them he could read sadness and desolation and despair—all behind the loveliness of a vitality that should have been sparkling with innocence and vivacity and the joyousness of youth.

She pulled the door wider.

'You had better come in while I dress,' she said.

'Thank you.'

M. Pinaud stepped into the great hall.

He had heard all about this fantastic house, but had never been inside. It was as if five hundred years of history had been suddenly turned back before his eyes.

The hall was complete, architecturally, as it had been when first used. Any restoration or repair had been accomplished so skilfully and so sympathetically, as to be unnoticeable. The solar, the minstrels' gallery, the two steep and ladder-like staircases, were all intact.

Two of the three fireplaces, one at each end, were exactly as he had imagined them to be. In each recess, on the opposite side of a pile of sawn and split logs, was a massive circular stand supporting several iron pokers and tongs. The third, the original one, had been left, unused and restored on its slabs of original stone in the centre of the hall, the smoke aperture in the beams above filled in.

Several beautiful Persian rugs mitigated the stark and bare coldness of the waxed flagstone floor and some deep tapestried wing-chairs of a later date added comfort and charm to the great room's austerity.

'Can you make coffee?'

He roused himself with a start from his somewhat understandable day-dreams of envy and smiled.

'Yes. I have even been complimented.'

'Good. I need coffee. You will find the kitchen and everything you require through that end door there. Don't look so worried—you won't have to rub two sticks together to make a fire. The kitchen has been modernized. I won't be long.'

She turned to the staircase.

M. Pinaud started forward and then stopped. So much had happened, so much had been unexpected that the one obvious question had not even been asked.

'But, Madame—'

She paused with one hand on the rail. How beautiful she was, he thought—how dainty and how graceful and how charming.

'Lorette, not Madame,' she said patiently.

'Lorette, then—where is your husband?'

For a moment she did not answer. The great room seemed to glow with golden light as the morning sun rose higher with ever-increasing power and warmth outside the tall leaded windows. He wondered idly whether the birds had resumed their song. Here, inside the mighty thickness of stone walls and behind closed panes, there was only silence.

Her features were composed and calm as she replied.

'In prison—in the local gaol at Pontlieu. They came for him soon after we notified them. I will tell you all about it when I come down.'

Then, pulling up her robe with one hand, she ran lightly up the steep stairs and left him alone.

All you seem to have been doing, Pinaud, ever since that telephone call, he reflected moodily, is swilling coffee and smoking cigarettes. This will not help your gastric juices. You will get a pain in your guts. Do not be surprised if an ulcer is forming even now in your outraged and abused intestines. Now perhaps he will listen to you and buy you a new car. Now perhaps he will realize that you were right.

As he thought, he worked quickly and efficiently. He put water and milk on the electric cooker to boil, he found a tablecloth and table-napkins in a drawer, crockery and cutlery in a cupboard, butter in the refrigerator and rolls in the larder.

Being fairly well domesticated through sheer force of circumstance and taking a pride, because of his very nature, in doing any task well, he soon had the table attractively laid, the milk steaming gently and the coffee percolating vigorously and aromatically. He even found a shallow bowl of pansies on a window-shelf in the hall which he transferred to the kitchen table.

Then he sat down, lit another cigarette, and waited for Lorette.

What a situation, he thought. What a shambles—the head of the *Sûreté* in a local gaol. It was unbelievable. And yet it had happened. It was a fact. He remembered that the jurisdiction of the Paris *Sûreté* did not extend beyond the bounds of the city. Here in Pontlieu the *Sûreté Nationale* was supreme. Even so, this was strange, although he had to admit that the circumstantial evidence was overwhelming—M. le Chef was obviously the logical suspect.

Yet had he himself arrived on time, things might well have been different. His request for a new car would now be impossible to refuse. He had surely proved his point.

Mind you, Pinaud, he told himself sternly, it would be advisable to use a little tact in relation to this matter. Remember that when you go to see him. However srongly you feel about the subject, the local gaol is hardly the place to introduce it. There are even more important things to do first. Such as getting him out.

The door opened and Lorette came into the kitchen. She wore a pale blue linen frock so beautifully cut that it appeared simple, and with her shoulder-length golden hair looked about seventeen. Until one looked at her eyes, M. Pinaud thought.

For a moment, as she stood there and contemplated the table and his efforts, she smiled. The lines of tension and strain vanished and her features were transfigured. This was the first time he had seen her smile, he thought.

He pulled out a chair and held it while she sat down. Then he went to fetch the coffee-pot.

'Now tell me what happened,' he said gently. 'Eat and drink and talk.'

'I came back from my uncle's house in Charanton suddenly and unexpectedly,' she began quietly. 'Not because I wanted to spy on him or anything like that, but simply because I felt I wanted to be home.'

Behind the quiet words he could sense a bitterness and a sadness that were tragic in their intensity.

Then she laughed, shortly and hardly.

'But this is not the time to talk about our marriage. You want to know what happened.'

'If you feel you would like to talk about it,' he told her gravely, 'I shall be honoured by your confidence.'

She shook her head.

'No. This is not the time. There is too much to do. I arrived here late—soon after he had telephoned you—and found him in a dreadful state. He had gone out for a short walk across the park to see his friend M'sieu Poidevin, who lives nearby, and when he came back he found her dead in the bed.'

She paused for a moment and then added:

'In my bed.'

And again the bitterness and sadness seemed to surge up behind the tension, the feeling and the emotion in her voice. M. Pinaud, with rare tact, did not say anything. His silence was more sympathetic than any words could have been.

In a short while she continued.

'Charles would not do anything. He insisted on waiting until you came. He said—not once but a hundred times—that you would know what to do. We waited and waited—and still you did not come.'

M. Pinaud opened his mouth to speak and then closed it again. The past was done. It was useless even to discuss it. He resented keenly the injustice of it all—her words implied that he had been at fault—but this was not the time for recrimination.

'We waited until I felt that I could not stand it any longer. I knew I would begin to scream if we did not get that body out of the house. I am afraid it was all my fault—I persuaded him in the end to telephone the police and tell them what had happened. At last—when you still did not come—he finally agreed. I realize now—now that it is too late—that I was wrong.'

'Why?'

'Because Louis Salvan, the inspector here in Pontlieu, is a narrow-minded bigot who hates Charles. He is nearing retirement age and has spent all his life waiting for the promotion that never came. This has made him sour and bitter and jealous. He saw his chance and took it, I suppose. He came with two policemen, guns out and the siren screaming, arrested Charles on suspicion of murder and took him to gaol.'

For a moment there was silence. Then she laughed again, still without mirth.

'I suppose I ought to be thankful that they took the evidence away as well. At least I got some sleep—knowing that the body was no longer in the house.'

M. Pinaud finished the last roll—she had not eaten one—drained his seventh cup of coffee and stood up.

'Thank you,' he said quietly. 'I will go now and see this Inspector Salvan. Would you mind staying here until I come back?'

'Of course not. I shall have to buy another bed, but that can wait. There are plenty of others. This is my home. This house used to belong to my uncle—I was brought up here as a child.'

'Good. I will be as quick as I can.'

'I repeat,' said Inspector Salvan loudly and aggressively, 'you cannot see him. It is not possible to see him. No one can see him. He is a prisoner of the State, arrested on suspicion of first-degree murder. I would not permit such a thing.'

He was tall and thin, with a bulging round forehead and restless eyes. He contemplated M. Pinaud with active hostility, evident contempt and considerable distaste.

M. Pinaud carefully kept his tone reasonable, his features expressionless.

'But this is the chief of the Paris Sûreté—'

'I don't care if he is the Pope in Rome. To me he is just a man locked up on suspicion of murder. Very strong suspicion, I may tell you, completely justifying my procedure. He will be formally charged in due course. The circumstantial evidence against him is overwhelming. More than overwhelming—crushing.'

'Circumstantial evidence is known to be—'

'Not this time, M'sieu Pinaud—not this time. He was alone in his house with the girl. Housemaid he says. Housemaid my arse. Who wants a housemaid when one has such a wife? This is an absolute scandal. Everyone knows what goes on in that house. I call it disgusting. The rich think they can get away with anything—that their money can buy their own laws and command their own justice and set their own standards and—'

M. Pinaud considered that it was time he took a turn at interrupting, especially as this conversation was not getting them anywhere. The man was obviously a fanatic, riding his favourite hobby-horse with a vindictive and splenetic delight.

'Inspector Salvan,' he interposed firmly. 'You are entitled to your own opinions, although I fail to see your reasons for expressing them now. The fact remains that whatever has happened, this gentleman in your custody is still the chief of the Paris *Sûreté*.'

The inspector eyed him sullenly, but still obdurately.

'That may be. That I do not dispute. But he has no authority here.'

For a fleeting moment—brief and yet somehow terrible—hate and malignancy flared openly and nakedly in the hooded eyes. His voice changed and trembled with intensity as he spoke.

'Neither have you, M'sieu Pinaud. That is something you would do well to remember. You are another one of his type—smug and self-satisfied, arrogant and hypocritical. Your kind have never had to worry. You all stick together far too closely. What do you know of not being able to find work—day after day and week after week—and even for months—watching your savings get less and less, enduring the silent reproof and condemnation of your own children, sensing the secret contempt of your wife, feeling your very soul and manhood getting gradually rotten with the anxiety and the responsibility and the frustration of it all—have you ever known such things, M'sieu Pinaud? Has your employer ever felt the same?

'You come here from another world—a private and self-righteous world that has always been the same for you and your kind—and you don't understand. It would do you good if the bottom suddenly fell out of it—then perhaps you might learn. As others have had to learn—the hard way.'

He paused for a moment, and when he continued his voice was quieter, but none the less intense.

'As I said, neither he nor you have any authority here. I take my orders from the *Sûreté Nationale*—'

M. Pinaud's interruption was as sharp and as swift as the thrust of a sword.

'And are you obeying orders now—or acting on your own initiative?'

There was a long silence. The inspector's face seemed to close and become strangely set.

'That is my business,' he answered quietly. 'I only know that your chief is no longer in a position to be arrogant or have any influence. Or to take housemaids to bed when his wife is away. Or to receive visitors now. Let us leave it at that, M'sieu Pinaud.'

M. Pinaud realized that it was useless to threaten a man who was either only obeying his superior's orders, or if not, was acting within the strict interpretation of his own rights.

This was something he could not settle himself. This situation called for and needed intervention on a brigadier-general level, not that of a corporal.

'Very well,' he said quietly, carefully keeping his voice expressionless. 'I will be seeing you again, Inspector Salvan. Goodbye for now.'

'I need your help, Lorette,' he told her when he got back to the manor-house.

'Why—what happened?'

'You were right about Inspector Salvan. He refused to give me an interview with your husband. Either he is working off some personal grudge, or else he is obeying orders, which makes the affair even more complicated. In any case, we have to go over his head.'

'How?'

'I understand your uncle is the Duke of Charanton.'

'Yes.'

'He is a very influential man. I am sure he would be able to organize it. Could we go there to see him together? Would you introduce me so that I can ask for his help? I must see and talk to your husband.'

'Of course.'

Lorette had already turned towards the door. Now she paused as she spoke to him.

'I should have thought of that myself. My only excuse is that I was so upset by all this that I have not been able to think clearly. You are quite right. If anyone can help, it is Uncle Roland. He knows everyone. And—oh yes—he is a personal friend of Maître Mansard—'

'What—the great Mansard?' he interrupted quickly. 'The criminal lawyer in Paris?'

'Yes—do you know him?'

'No. But everyone knows of him, and his reputation. He is the best. Come on—why are we waiting?'

Outside the front door he gestured towards the Ferrari.

'May we go in your car?'

For a moment she hesitated.

'Yes—but why? I mean—what is the point—'

He looked at her and did not see her. He knew that the sunlight would be glinting like gold in the threads of her hair and that the gentian-blue eyes would be wide with astonishment and puzzlement, like those of a child—but he did not see her. He saw only with his imagination and his memory. He saw once again the wet flesh and the seductive contours of that magnificent body under the loose robe. And he knew that he could not tell her the real reason. He could not tell her the truth.

Within him they warred continuously, the man and the detective, sometimes as entities, sometimes immutably and inextricably fused in a complex interplay of character and nature that kept him in an often unbearable state of tension.

At the moment he did not know which one was predominant.

The brooding intensity of his stare vanished as he smiled and he lied swiftly and convincingly.

'Shall we say because I have never been in such a car before in my life—and would very much like to have the experience?'

She smiled faintly, but she did not laugh. He wondered if she believed him.

She walked on past his car.

'Come on, then—it is not locked. Would you like to drive?'

He shook his head and walked to the passenger seat.

'No, thank you. Some other time, perhaps.'

He got in, closing his door quietly with a decisive click. The other door banged and the engine whispered and roared into life and then throbbed impatiently with the characteristic crackle bubbling from its four gleaming exhausts.

M. Pinaud reached down on to the carpet and pulled up the tyre-lever.

'What on earth is this?'

Lorette let in the clutch and the car swept smoothly out of the courtyard.

'That,' she replied without taking her eyes off the road, 'that is a tyre-lever.'

He laughed.

'I know. I meant—what is a tyre-lever doing here on the floor?'

'It is kept there so that I can get at it quickly.'

'But surely that is extreme pessimism? With modern tyres such as these a puncture is very unlikely. Even if you should have one, there is a spare wheel. The wheel-brace and the jack on the floor I can understand—if you are in a hurry to get somewhere—but surely you will never have to remove the tyre from the wheel under normal—'

'That tyre-lever,' she interrupted calmly, driving carefully and slowly and concentrating entirely on what she was doing, 'has nothing to do with the car. It is a weapon. For self-defence. For protection.'

'Against whom?'

She lifted her foot from the accelerator and the car slowed. Then she turned her head and looked at him directly as she replied.

'Against all the queer types who so obviously want to be sitting where you are, M'sieu Pinaud, beside me in this beautiful car. I have seen the expression in their eyes and on their faces as they signal me for a lift. I am not a timid person, but what I see makes me feel sick and frightened. I usually drive with the top down. If I were obliged to stop or compelled to drive too slowly, an active man could easily jump in.'

She changed gear and the car picked up speed. Yet she still continued to drive carefully, competently and—at the wheel of such a car—with strange and unnatural slowness.

'I see what you mean,' he said, replacing the tyre-lever on the floor. 'I think you are quite right. Anyone as beautiful as you are should take every care and precaution. There are some strange people in the world today.'

He looked at her and saw that she was blushing at his compliment.

For the moment he put the matter from his mind. He had another problem to occupy it.

When one owned a car that was capable of a speed of well over three hundred kilometres an hour, and had an obvious enthusiast sitting in the passenger seat, surely it was contrary to human nature not to show, with justifiable and entirely understandable pride, something of what that car could do—to demonstrate some small measure of its performance—and not drive as if one were delivering milk.

And so, mostly in silence because he was preoccupied with his problem, they came to Charanton.

4

The town house of the noble family of Charanton was secluded, austere and magnificent.

M. Pinaud waited in a room of lofty and exquisite proportions, overlooking a walled garden whose belt of centuries-old trees completed the illusion that the house was in the heart of the country and not in the centre of a town—a room so beautifully, immaculately and tastefully furnished that he did not dare to smoke.

He waited patiently while Lorette went first into the study to tell her uncle what had happened.

'Didn't you telephone him last night?' M. Pinaud wanted to know when she asked if he would not mind waiting.

'No. This is my problem, not his. At least, that is what I thought last night. Now I realize that you are right—we need his help. I shall not be long.'

She was as good as her word. Whatever had to be said was completed quickly.

The Duke stood up politely behind his desk as she ushered M. Pinaud into the book-lined study, and then left them alone, closing the door quietly behind her.

He was a small man, neat and precise and impeccably clothed. He had noble and arresting features—the forehead high and lofty, the nose curved and dominant, the mobile mouth with its long upper-lip and down-curving corners strong and yet humorous and kindly. His eyes, beneath pouched and hooded lids, were wise and shrewd and calm with the absolute certainty of knowledge and power.

He could have been a small and insignificant figure, were it not for the magnificent brow and the dynamic intelligence of the deep-set eyes.

He held out his hand.

'Welcome to Charanton, M'sieu Pinaud,' he said cordially. 'And be generous enough to forgive my discourtesy in making you wait, but my niece had things to tell me. Please sit down.'

'Thank you, M'sieu le Duc,' replied M. Pinaud. 'There was no discourtesy. It was the natural thing to do.'

The Duke resumed his own seat behind the desk and smiled, briefly and suddenly, and his outstanding and forceful personality seemed to flood the room.

'You are kind—thank you. She also wanted very much to tell me about you yourself. I thought it far more satisfactory to see you separately.'

It was M. Pinaud's turn to smile.

'There is nothing I can add to what you already know from her', he said quietly.

The Duke's eyes grew sombre.

'No—of course not. But perhaps we can discuss this— this impossible situation a little more freely without her.'

He paused. M. Pinaud said nothing, but waited for him to continue. The Duke leaned back in his chair and looked at him speculatively.

'Do you believe he did it?'

'No—of course not.'

'You do not hesitate.'

'No. I have no doubts. I cannot believe he would do a thing like that.'

'But—sexual release—and perhaps abnormal gratification—to a man of his age—'

'Nonsense. He is being framed.'

'You are loyal. That is something rare in the world today.'

'His private life and marriage are no concern of mine. But I have known him, worked with him and respected him for many years.'

'Then we must help him.'

'That is why I came.'

Again there was a silence and again the Duke's eyes grew sombre.

'I admire your sentiments, M'sieu Pinaud—but I wish you had not come.'

'Why?'

'Your appeal—and the way you have presented it—

place me in a difficult position. You must understand one thing, M'sieu Pinaud—I love my niece, as all the family of Charanton love each other—and even more. There is nothing—I repeat nothing—that I would not do if necessary to ensure her happiness.'

It was not difficult for M. Pinaud to wait and not answer. Behind his impassive expression his mind was racing with all the implications of what he had just heard.

'And now you are asking me to use whatever influence and power I have—which you must know is not inconsiderable—to save a marriage which has been a tragedy from the day it started.'

'I did not know that.'

'No. Few people did. They have both dissembled and dissimulated, very successfully. Lorette because she has the pride of all the Charantons, Charles because he likes being married to a Charanton and the niece of a Duke. Of late his infidelities have grown worse—but I am old and wise enough to know that Lorette may be partly to blame for this. A marriage is such a close and intimate relationship that when it goes wrong blame can never belong entirely to one side. Besides—to a happy and vigorous marriage— infidelities are straws, blown by the wind of circumstance, completely powerless, entirely insignificant.'

Something he read in M. Pinaud's eyes brought that brief and sudden smile to his lips for the second time.

'You are a good listener, M'sieu Pinaud. You have a quality of sympathetic silence which I have only met once before in my life. Perhaps that is why I am talking to you so freely—I do not know.

'But you tell me you have known Charles for years. And now you have met Lorette. You can form your own impressions and draw your own conclusions. She is young and romantic. She met Charles when she was on the rebound from an unfortunate affair—a boy and girl romance that somehow endured—and ended in tragedy. He was killed in a car accident. Here was an older man—with all an older man's charm and experience and sympathy—here was the glamour of the Paris *Sûreté* and all the thrills of the almost incredible adventures he took such a pride in recounting.'

For the third time the smile touched his lips.

'You realize, don't you, M'sieu Pinaud—that you yourself have been largely responsible for this marriage?'

'I? How?'

'These were your adventures, your exploits and your triumphs he never tired of telling. He sat at his desk and set the wheels in motion—but you were the one who had to go out and follow wherever they led. He lived your astonishing exploits vicariously. He found satisfaction and fulfilment in whatever you did and therefore took perhaps a little more than his share of the credit.

'All this—somewhat naturally—made a great impression on Lorette. She is young and therefore an idealist, and she was swept off her feet. But there is a limit to what the young can stand. It is only when one grows old that one learns to endure. I could see that they were incompatible from the start.'

He finished speaking, sighed and lifted the receiver from the telephone on his desk. With the other hand he pressed the bell.

'Good morning, madame. Would you get me Maître Mansard in Paris, please. Yes, it is Saturday—he will be at home. Thank you.'

He replaced the receiver. There was a knock on the door.

'Come in,' he said.

A large and portly and yet still powerful individual stood on the threshold. He wore an open frock-coat and around his paunch a huge leather belt hung with keys. He bowed slightly, with great dignity, and waited in silence.

'Maître Mansard is a busy man, M'sieu Pinaud. His line is usually engaged, even at home. Permit me to offer you a glass of wine while we are waiting for the call.'

M. Pinaud thought of his gastric juices with trepidation and considerable qualms. It was early in the day, even for one of his experience, to start drinking wine, although he had once seen an army colonel, with a skin like blue leather, drinking absinthe for breakfast.

Then, in the same instant, he dismissed the thought as mean and unworthy and pitiful. It was not every day that a humble detective was invited to take wine with a Duke. And his skin was not—at least not yet—like blue leather.

'Thank you, M'sieu le Duc—it is extremely kind of you.'

'Three years ago we had a Burgandy which some freak combination of sun and rain made unique—a throw-back— a wine that happens once in a hundred years. The experts tell me I am too far north for Burgundy, but in my small vineyards I delight in proving them wrong. I shall welcome your opinion, M'sieu Pinaud—as I understand that you are something of a connoisseur. A bottle, if you please, Jules, and some dry biscuits. It is a little early in the day.'

'In here, M'sieu le Duc?'

The wine-steward's voice was expressionless, his manner faultlessly polite and respectful, and yet in his attitude and bearing he managed to scream—in perfect silence—a definite and outraged reproof.

'Yes, Jules. In here. We are waiting for a telephone call from Paris.'

'Very well, M'sieu le Duc.'

The door closed behind him.

'Jules does not approve of drinking wine in a study,' remarked the Duke dryly. 'He is one of the old school. Sometimes he can be very trying. Often he is infuriating. But I forgive him—as I would forgive many others like him—because of his loyalty. He was brought up in a tradition of service and devotion which the world has forgotten today. To me in consequence it is a poorer and a meaner place—but then I am somewhat naturally biassed.'

He paused for a moment and looked at M. Pinaud with a strange intensity.

'Jules would do anything for me—anything I asked. He would not even pause to think whether it were difficult or dangerous or even criminal. The fact that I asked him to do it would be enough.'

He sighed shortly.

'Such men are rare. I am fortunate in having grown up surrounded by them.'

'The world has changed,' ventured M. Pinaud, hoping that he did not sound too sententious.

The rare smile touched the corners of that mobile mouth.

'Not in this lost backwater, M'sieu Pinaud. Elsewhere—yes. And has lost thereby. But here in Charanton we still live in the traditions of the past, and with all their faults and injustices, our lives not only have purpose and meaning but are infinitely richer and more dignified. This I believe and have proved.'

The telephone rang. He picked up the receiver.

'Hullo—yes. Albert? How are you? Roland here. Yes, fine. Look—I want you to do something for me. Good. This may be difficult, but it has got to be done. Charles is locked up in the gaol at Pontlieu—yes. Don't ask me. A man called Salvan. He may be within his rights—that is for you to sort out. But there are exceptions even to rights, as you know. Yes. Quite. Exactly. I suggest you go at once to see Dumarchais yourself—don't telephone—and put it to him nicely and politely at first. That's right. See his re-action. Yes. Then tell him that I and the Minister and the President if necessary will be at his house this afternoon, if he feels he needs a little more encouragement. Exactly. Charles, after all, apart from being a relation of mine by marriage, is the head of the Paris *Sûreté,* and I feel that there are certain courtesies which you and I and all of us would like to see observed. Yes. I agree with you.'

For a long moment he listened without speaking, his face grave, his manner attentive, and then continued.

'A bad one, I'm afraid. Murder. Circumstantial evidence. M'sieu Pinaud here thinks he has been framed. Yes. I had heard rumours of pressure. But all this can be sorted out in a decent and civilized manner when he is out on bail. I want a telephone call from Dumarchais to this Salvan right away—while you are with him, if possible. Good. I knew I could rely on you. Thank you very much. Let me know as soon as you can—I am waiting here with M'sieu Pinaud. Goodbye.'

He replaced the receiver very carefully and quietly.

M. Pinaud felt inwardly troubled. He had just heard the manifestations of power—of a power untramelled and unimpaired after centuries of attack and disruption, a power transcending the law, a power that was an oligarchy—unseen and seldom apparent—in its omnipotence. The implications were frightening.

Jules knocked on the door and entered the room, carrying a tray with rather more care and reverence than a mother would accord to a new-born baby.

He set it on the desk and poured the wine with a painstaking care and attention which precluded any speech. Obediently they waited in silence.

Then, when he had left the room, his bearing proud with the consciousness of a task well done, every line of his rigid back proclaiming his unspoken condemnation of this violation of his traditional principles, the Duke motioned towards the tray.

'Help yourself, M'sieu Pinaud. Tell me what you think of it.'

M. Pinaud raised his glass courteously in salutation and drank, slowly and carefully. Then he drank again. Then he set the glass back on the tray and tried to find words to describe what he felt.

The wine seemed to caress his tongue, his mouth and his palate like a fire behind a cool velvet glove. It coursed down his throat like a warm and spreading liquid hand, which opened out and unfolded and flowed round about every part of his stomach, surging over them into waves of radiant comfort, whose ecstasy emanated fumes he could actually feel swirling back again the way they had come to ascend to his brain, clarifying, accentuating and stimulating all his senses.

The Duke had refilled his glass. He drank again, this time in disbelief, this time to convince himself that he had been mistaken, that he had imagined all these things and that the wild flights of his imagination had no solid foundation.

He drank in disbelief and was convinced. The second glass was even better than the first. To prove this it seemed only fair to finish it.

Then he leaned back in his chair and spoke with a fitting solemnity.

'You must forgive me, M'sieu le Duc. There are words in my mind, but I could not express them. I still cannot express them. I have never tasted such a wonderful wine in my life before.'

'I am glad. And I am pleased you appreciate it. There is nothing to forgive—it has this effect on most people. Take your time and enjoy it—we may have to wait some time for Maître Mansard's call. Try a biscuit. There are plenty more bottles in the cellar.'

He refilled M. Pinaud's glass and sipped at his own. M. Pinaud drank again.

Somewhere at the back of his mind, beneath all the waves and the fumes and the ecstasy, he seemed to hear the faint note of a warning bell.

You should not be sitting here, Pinaud, he told himself sternly, drinking wine at this hour of the morning, when you are engaged on what may well prove to be the most difficult and complicated case of your career. You will remember—while you are still capable of recollection—the evident disapproval of Jules, who obviously had absorbed the lesson that drinking wine in unorthodox places inevitably leads to drinking wines at unorthodox times. You will also observe—while you still retain the powers and the faculty of observation—that your host the Duke is sipping at his wine while you are swallowing yours. And for a very good reason. He knows exactly what his vineyards have produced.

He smiled benignly and forgivingly at his own intolerance, emptied his glass and ate a dry biscuit, which tasted more delicious than any biscuit he had ever eaten.

He addressed himself again, but this time with a little more sympathy and kindness. On the other hand, Pinaud, you must never lose your sense of proportion. The opportunity of drinking a Duke's own wine in the company of the Duke himself, is not given every day to a mere detective. You have been both honoured and privileged, and in addition this man—even if and although he is a Duke—is helping you. There are exceptions to every rule. And to cavil and carp and find fault is usually the sign of a small and mean mind.

He watched the Duke refill his glass with a detached and benevolent approval and then spoke quietly.

'Tell me, M'sieu le Duc, at what time did your niece leave last night to go home?'

The Duke frowned, trying to remember.

'I am afraid I have no idea. I had no reason to check. Some time after dinner—no, it was quite late, I believe. She tried to telephone twice—she just thought she would ask if he was all right—but there was no answer.

'Then she began to get worried—she has been moody and upset lately—and suddenly decided that she ought to go back herself. She is very much a creature of impulse. She jumped in her car and drove off.'

There was silence for a moment. When the Duke spoke again his voice had an edge of bitterness.

'I did not argue. I did not interfere. It is her problem, and therefore one that she must solve herself. I can only watch her unhappiness and grow sad as I remember how she used to be and see how she has changed. She is no longer the same person. Those who have children, M'sieu Pinaud, must always give hostages to fortune.'

The telephone rang. He picked up the receiver and listened intently for some moments.

'Good. Thank you very much, Albert. I knew I could count on you. M'sieu Pinaud will take it up from there. I will keep in touch and let you know what happens. Yes. Goodbye.'

He replaced the receiver and stood up. M. Pinaud began to rise, but the Duke waved him back into his chair.

'Please—do not get up. I was only going to fetch Lorette. There is still a little left in the bottle—there is no point in keeping it.'

He filled M. Pinaud's glass almost to the brim and laid the empty bottle carefully in its basket.

'Well,' he continued, 'as you probably gathered, that is that. He can come out on bail. The amount is not yet fixed, but that is not important. They must know that Lorette and I can both sign cheques to meet it.'

The door opened and Lorette came into the room.

M. Pinaud stood up quickly.

'Lorette—I was just coming to tell you,' said the Duke. 'Maître Mansard has this moment telephoned. Charles can come out on bail.'

She looked at the bottle on the tray.

'No wonder Jules looked so upset,' she said coolly. 'You know how he feels about this morning drinking.'

The Duke looked at her severely.

'That is only because it denies him the chance of showing off,' he said. Beneath the quiet voice there was an edge of steel. 'Because his family have held the position for seven generations, that does not give him the right to tell me what to do and when to drink. Is that all you have to say—about Charles?'

'No,' she replied slowly. 'I am glad—for his sake. I only wanted time to think. Now that I have thought, I would prefer to remain here with you, Uncle Roland, if you do not mind. I will run you back to Pontlieu, M'sieu Pinaud, but I would rather not stay.'

'Why not?' asked M. Pinaud quietly.

'Now that Charles can go home and has you to help him, he does not need me any—'

'Nonsense. This is just the time he does need you.'

'I have loved every stone of that house all my life. Now I feel I cannot stand it any more.'

'This thing began in the manor-house and it will probably end there. That is where you should be. Besides, running away from trouble never helped anyone. To find a solution you must face it.'

For a long time they looked at each other in silence. The Duke said nothing. Then suddenly she smiled.

'All right. You win. Just wait while I get my gloves.'

The Duke shook hands cordially and told him to keep in touch.

M. Pinaud walked very carefully towards the red Ferrari, remembering thankfully that most police-stations, whatever their situation, could usually provide a pot of black coffee. It had been quite a morning.

5

Inspector Salvan's manner had changed considerably.

'Some people have influence,' he sneered sullenly by way of greeting.

As he did not like rudeness, M. Pinaud decided to drive the point home.

'Yes,' he agreed cheerfully. 'This is a fact advisable to remember, especially when thinking of one's career, for example. Now can I see him?'

'Of course. He is free to go out on bail, as arranged by Maître Mansard.'

And now behind the sullenness there was an awe and respect amounting almost to reverence. People who could achieve the impossible, types who could work miracles, rated highly in the inspector's estimation.

'We shall see about that later,' replied M. Pinaud coolly. 'First of all I want to see him. And then I would like to examine the body. Where is she?'

'In the morgue, m'sieu. It is in this building.'

'Good.'

'I will bring him here, and you can use this office.'

'Thank you.'

He thought swiftly. Now would be a good opportunity to take advantage of the inspector's sudden conversion and test his newly acquired benevolence to the full.

'Oh—and yes,' he added. 'Would you be kind enough to send us in a pot of black coffee, very hot and very strong—if it is not too much trouble.'

'Certainly, m'sieu.'

Not for nothing had Maître Mansard established his fame and reputation.

The inspector left him alone, returned in very short time and ushered M. le Chef deferentially into the room. Then he went out closing the door behind him.

M. le Chef sat down heavily at the desk. M. Pinaud was shocked at the change in his appearance. He looked drawn

and tired and years older. His voice was slow and reproach-
ful.

'I am glad to see you at last, Pinaud. It is only an hour's
drive. You said you would come at once.'

M. Pinaud looked at him and felt pity and compassion.
He decided not to go into details about his car. On yet
another occasion he had been proved right and other people wrong, but this was neither the time nor the place to
make a fuss about it. Like his salary, this was a sore point,
but every subject gained stature from being introduced
aptly and appropriately, and this was now definitely impossible.

'It is good to see you, m'sieu,' he said carefully, his tone
successfully masking his feelings. 'My car broke down and
I did not arrive until early this morning. I came here at
once, but Inspector Salvan would not allow me to see you.
I had to go to Charanton, to your uncle-in-law the Duke.
He persuaded Maître Mansard to bring some pressure.
This is obviously all part of what you were telling me
yesterday.'

There, he reflected with satisfaction, lighting a cigarette,
perhaps a little defiantly, just to show that he was no longer
in that magnificent room on the second floor but in a very
shabby office next to the local gaol—there, leave it at that.
A fairly factual account, apart from details of breakfast
with his wife, which obviously were completely irrelevant.
It should take his mind back to his own troubles. He has
enough worries at present without having to think about
my car as well.

'Yes,' said M. le Chef gloomily. 'That is what I said.
Very powerful influences.'

He looked as though he were going to brood. M. Pinaud
decided he had better not give him the chance. The last
conversation on that subject had produced singularly little
results.

There was a knock on the door. The desk-sergeant came
in with coffee on a tray. M. Pinaud thanked him politely
and poured out two cups.

'Now then,' he said, drinking his eagerly and burning his

throat, 'I want to know exactly what happened. Tell me all about it.'

M. le Chef eyed his coffee as if it were something flushed away from an operating theatre and did not touch the cup.

'Well, as I told you on the telephone, I went out some time between nine and ten for a short—'

'Why?'

'What do you mean—why?'

'Surely it is not normal to go out for a walk—any walk—whether short, medium or long—in the middle of fornication? Smoke—yes. Drink—quite usual. Switch on music—fairly common. Sing—frequently. Dance—not unknown, in the nude. Telephone to cancel an appointment—understandable. But to go out for a walk—incomprehensible.'

M. le Chef showed what was for him remarkable patience.

'Poidevin telephoned as we were eating and asked me to go over to his house for a few moments. Some advice he wanted about his garden. I always go out for a walk in the evening. The exercise does me good. Last night I thought I would combine the two. It was as simple as that.'

'Did you go to M'sieu Poidevin?'

'No, I did not. I walked across the park almost as far as his house and then suddenly decided that it was too late and too dark to talk about gardens. I changed my mind and thought that this morning would do just as well.'

He paused and smiled a little sadly.

'This morning was somewhat different.'

'I see. Go on, please. Leave this for now—we can come back to it later.'

'I returned to the house, went upstairs and found her like that in the bed.'

He shivered suddenly, although the office was warm.

'I think you will agree with me—even after a lifetime of dealing with violent death, you don't understand or realize what these things mean until they happen to you yourself.

'At first I panicked. I nearly lost my head. I had mad thoughts of burying the body in the garden and telling everyone that she had left unexpectedly. She was only a temporary help—engaged for a few days while my wife went to visit her relations.

'Mercifully they did not last. I had a good stiff drink of brandy and started to think rationally. Then I telephoned you. I knew that was the right thing to do. Once you came everything would be all right.'

He paused for a moment and sighed heavily.

'You did not appear—but Lorette came home unexpectedly. That was something I needed like a hole in my head. I was not expecting her until tomorrow. We waited and waited, but still you did not come. As soon as I had told her, Lorette wanted to telephone the police. She maintained that it was the only thing to do. I argued with her for a long time, knowing that it was essential to talk to you first, but we kept on waiting and you did not come and she kept insisting—until in the end I gave in and did what she wanted.'

M. Pinaud successfully—though not without difficulty—resisted the impulse to say 'I told you so' and contented himself with repeating 'I see' to show that he was thinking only about what he was being told.

'After that, I was finished. This Inspector Salvan hates me. He did not hesitate for one moment. He would not even listen to me.'

'In all fairness to him,' said M. Pinaud quietly. 'The circumstantial evidence is bad. You were alone in the house—'

'Yes, I know. We employ a chauffeur-gardener called Bayard who also does the odd jobs. He lives in a flat above the garage. But he was out as well. He usually goes out every evening once his work is done.'

'If he does not live inside the house, then as a witness he does not count.'

'No, I suppose not,' agreed M. le Chef heavily. 'As you say, I was alone in the house.'

For a long moment there was silence. Then M. Pinaud leaned forward in his chair and spoke, very quietly and yet with great intensity.

'Did you kill her?'

M. le Chef's reply was swift and indignant.

'Of course not. Why should I? I did not engage her to kill her. She had other duties.'

'That may be. But these things sometimes happen, especially with older people. As you took the trouble to point out to me yesterday morning, m'sieu, neither of us is getting any younger. And the casebook of your files will tell you how often it can happen—particularly during actions of extreme and unaccustomed sexual frenzy, such as might well occur during copulation with a young girl.'

M. Pinaud's voice remained quiet. But now as he spoke it grew thoughtful and sad as well, and his eyes grew sombre and dark with the pain of memories he would rather have forgotten.

M. le Chef, however, was far too pre-occupied with his own troubles to notice any of this. He hardly gave M. Pinaud time to finish before he exploded with a violence and a vehemence which proved that his mercurial temperament was already well on the road to recovery.

'Bah. Rot. Cock. Nonsense. Of course not. Ridiculous. These things may have happened, as you say and as the files can prove—but I can tell you, Pinaud, that they certainly do not happen to me.'

'Why not? How can you be so sure? You realize that you probably would not even remember—'

'Nonsense. Balls. Tripe. Fiddlesticks. Lunacy.

'In the first place, I do not normally keep heavy instruments—of the type that killed her—by the bed for the purpose of intercourse. I confess to a perfectly healthy appetite occasionally for a little deviation from the normal, but again I am neither a sadist, nor a masochist, nor a pervert.

'In the second place, your postulation of unaccustomed frenzy completely wrecks and demolishes your theory by itself, if ever it did apply to me, for the simple reason that —as you probably have gathered by now—sexual activity is by no means an unaccustomed pleasure to me. I believe in constant exercise, of every muscle.

'And in the third place, even if your wrecked and demolished theory were correct, then surely it would have been consistent, within the average of all your premises, to strangle her and not batter her to death with a heavy instrument which no amount of searching would ever have found lying handy in my bedroom.'

He finally paused, and again for a long moment there was silence. M. Pinaud sat motionless, deep in thought.

This was good enough. If his friend said he was innocent, then that was sufficient. One did not argue, nor pursue the matter any further. One forgot evidence and procedure and began to look elsewhere. In this manner and with this tradition he had been brought up. Friendship implied implicit confidence and trust, or else there could be no meaning in the word.

If there happened to be so much that was incomprehensible in a situation where a man, married to someone as lovely as Lorette, could nevertheless engage a young housemaid and take her to his bed—then this just had to be accepted as something that concerned only the people involved, something that in consequence was not his business, and therefore something that did not need to be understood.

'Yes,' he said at last, slowly and thoughtfully. 'Someone made a bad mistake there. If they had intended to implicate you and frame you for this type of murder, she should have been strangled, as you said.'

On the other hand, his thoughts raced with the quickness of light, if someone had killed in a sudden madness of rage, such a choice of weapon might have been natural. And if someone had killed deliberately, so that M. le Chef would be implicated and frightened and perhaps even taught a well deserved lesson, such a choice of weapon would be essential, to ensure that there would be no risk— employing the finest defence that money could buy—of him being found guilty and convicted.

He could imagine and hear the ringing tones of Maître Mansard's blistering and unanswerable éloquence in the courtroom as clearly as he had heard his own voice a moment ago—'And is it likely, members of the jury, that a figure as respected and as wealthy as my client, able to surround himself with every luxury, comfort and convenience that money can buy—you have seen the photographs of his magnificent home—is it likely or even believable that to embellish the furnishings of that beautiful bedroom he would have added—to the cupboards and wardrobes filled with priceless silk and linen, *haute-couture* models and hand-tailored suits—or on the Persian rugs to enhance their exquisite weave—a tyre-lever or a poker, a spanner, a wrench or a hammer—the only type of weapon, as our learned medical expert has explained so skilfully and so carefully to us, consistent with the injuries inflicted on this unfortunate girl's skull?'

A pause for the well-known and histrionic flinging back of the long mane of hair in that traditional gesture of defiance and then the quiet and contemptuous whisper which so often evoked tumultuous applause before the gavels had a chance to strike—'Of course it is not likely. It is ridiculous.'

All these thoughts and images raced through his mind with that instantaneous wonder which is the miracle of imagination.

Aloud he continued to speak, after only a momentary pause.

'Come back now to the fact that, for whatever reason, you did go out and leave her alone. Since you did not do it—then you are being framed. You remember what you told me yesterday morning in your office. We both know why. My job is to find out who.'

'Of course. But it will not be easy.'

M. Pinaud looked at him sombrely. Perhaps it would be too easy. Perhaps it would be better not to find out. Would he be able to face the truth?

'Someone must have been watching the house, waiting for me to go out, to provide the opportunity. My new neighbour Poidevin—'

'New neighbour?' repeated M. Pinaud, interrupting him swiftly. 'How can you have a new neighbour? I thought you owned all the countryside around here.'

For the first time a smile touched M. le Chef's lips.

'Not quite. There was a derelict barn on the other side of the park. It had been abandoned and disused for years

and last winter the roof began to fall to pieces and became
an eyesore. So we got the local man to rebuild on the
foundations, which were still sound, and transform it into
a house. This he did, very successfully. Poidevin was due
to retire. We spoke about it in town. He came down here
one day to look, approved without hesitation and moved
in last month.'

'I see. What were you going to say about him?'

'What—oh, yes. He might have seen someone strange
hanging about before it got dark. You should ask him.
From his front windows he can see our house.'

'I will. From what you said, you usually take this short
walk in the evening. Therefore anyone watching would
have seen you go out.'

'Yes.'

'Very well. Come to the morgue with me, if you please,
m'sieu. I want to examine the body very carefully. You
may be able to remember something about her, something—'

'I would rather not, if you don't mind, Pinaud. I had
enough of looking at her last night.'

'All right. As you wish. It will not take long. Inspector
Salvan said the morgue is in the same building. You sit
here then and wait for me, and try to think of anything
about this girl that was unusual or different from the
others.'

His hands trembled as he pulled back the sheet. The
shocking violence of the mutilation seemed to trigger off a
resultant violence of emotion—what kind of person, in
their right mind, would do such a thing to the head of a
young girl?

On the other hand, he thought, murderers, at the actual
moment of execution of their crimes, were seldom in their
right minds. And there had not been much time. The
murder had to be done at once. M. le Chef was out, but
no one knew how long or how quick he would be. Stran-
gling a young and healthy person, without specialized
knowledge of nerve-centres, could sometimes be a difficult

and lengthy process and hence too risky. A heavy instrument was the ideal weapon; it could be concealed behind one's back while approaching the bed. This would have given the advantage of surprise and the quickness of achievement with one blow.

In spite of the terrible injuries, he could see that she had once been beautiful.

He pulled the sheet down further. Her body too, had been beautiful, small and firm and exquisitely proportioned. He judged her to have been young, in her early teens, and yet she had already borne a child. Her hands were delicate and finely boned, the fingertips soft and unmarked—not the hands of a housemaid.

He replaced the sheet gently, sighing at the pity and the waste and the tragedy of it all.

Then he washed his hands at the sink, lit a cigarette and walked back along the corridors to rejoin M. le Chef.

He found him not sitting down, but pacing to and fro impatiently within the narrow confines of the room.

'Well?' he asked quickly.

M. Pinaud replied with another question.

'Did you remember anything?'

M. le Chef sat down.

'No, I am afraid not. She was just another girl, more beautiful and perhaps better educated than some of the others. Her references said that she had been with some doctor in Charanton.'

'References can be forged.'

'Why?'

'She was no housemaid.'

M. le Chef frowned thoughtfully.

'Probably not. She did not do much work and what she did was no good. But it was only for a few days, so I did not bother. But then why—'

'She was planted here—for a specific purpose.'

M. le Chef turned pale.

'You mean—to be murdered? But that is horrible.'

M. Pinaud nodded thoughtfully.

'I know. To implicate you, certainly. Whether she was

to have been murdered as part of the plan—I don't know. Perhaps something went wrong. This is getting more and more complicated.'

He paused and suddenly seemed to make up his mind.

'Look, m'sieu—I must get back. I have people to see. I will keep in touch so that—'

'What do you mean, Pinaud—keep in touch? What the devil do you mean? Can't I come out? Inspector Salvan said that Maître Mansard had arranged bail.'

'I know. That is quite true. But you must stay here. It would be wiser to stay here.'

'Why? What are you talking about?'

'For safety. Because your life is still in danger. If they are prepared to kill in order to frame you for murder, then they will stop at nothing. You come out and go home and you could have an unfortunate accident. That is so easy to arrange.'

'But—'

'Far better to put up with this discomfort and inconvenience for another day or two. It is not worth the risk, believe me. Here you are safe. You are locked up and guarded—and therefore you are safe. Here they can't touch you or get at you.'

'Well,' said M. le Chef dubiously. 'If you put it like that—'

'I do put it like that,' replied M. Pinaud swiftly and cheerfully. 'That, m'sieu, is the only way it can be put. This is a situation with only one solution. Goodbye for now. I will come back to see you as soon as I can.'

Inspector Salvan stared, convinced that he was dealing with a madman, but his career as an opportunist had taught him that a madman who wielded such influence in high places must at all costs be placated, and therefore he did not argue, but conducted a slightly dazed M. le Chef civilly back to his cell.

Now amongst his detractors, there have been people small and petty-minded enough to suggest that M. Pinaud deliberately distorted the situation, exaggerated its dangers and purposely played upon M. le Chef's fears—for he was not a man of great physical courage—purely and simply so that he could be alone with Lorette in the manor-house. To these unfounded and malicious innuendos his chronicler (who is concerned solely with the truth) can only recall, not without bitterness, how often malice and envy have poisoned the lives of the great.

6

Her eyes were the blue of gentians in the sunlight. Her hair, each time she moved her head, reminded him of corn rippling and waving in the sweep of an invisible wind. And her body, taut and eager and lovely under its thin covering, set the blood pulsing and throbbing through his veins.

He told her most of what had happened. She listened attentively and in complete silence, without asking any questions. Even the news that he had advised M. le Chef to remain in the gaol, for his own safety's sake, aroused no comment, elicited no remark.

Then she leaned back in her chair and clasped her hands around one silk-clad knee.

'I left Charles one day last week to visit my uncle and aunt,' she said quietly and unexpectedly. 'You have met my uncle. You had probably heard of him before you met him. You will no doubt realize—most people have no difficulty in understanding—that with such a family there are certain duties and obligations which are so natural as to become inevitable. It is just this sense of cohesion which has enabled the great families of France to endure throughout centuries.'

She paused and laughed a little ruefully.

'I am afraid that is something which Charles has never been able or willing to accept.'

She paused again. M. Pinaud, with a rare sympathy, waited in silence. She was not interested in his comments. She had something to say. She wanted to talk. All he had to do was to listen.

'You will have gathered, M'sieu Pinaud, that our marriage has been a failure. It has been ruined by the very things that should have made it a success. Charles is and always has been dedicated to his career. He has done the hard work all his life. Now, with my money and the power and influence of my family's name—which as you have seen is not inconsiderable—he could have set the seal of success on all his efforts.'

Once more she paused and sighed.

'But his pride would not allow him. He has got some idea in his head he must win by himself—alone—in spite of our help, not because of it.'

Here she smiled wistfully.

'He finds it so hard to understand—and yet it is all so simple. He and my uncle can make no communication—they could be speaking a different language. When you have it all, the only problem is to keep it—not to go mad trying to get more. Two views that are incompatible and poles apart. He has resented my visits ever since I made the first one, and invited him to come with me. He refused, and has refused ever since. His excuse is that he is too busy, that he has too much work to do. He even quoted you on several occasions—'

'Me?' interrupted M. Pinaud, ungrammatically but with great interest.

'Yes—as an excuse. You always kept him so busy he said—your cases were so remarkable, your exploits so fantastic, that he could not afford to be away from the office even for one day, because you might telephone and demand that something vital be done at once and without delay.'

As if in a great blaze of light, M. Pinaud remembered swiftly all the many and different occasions on which he had telephoned M. le Chef in the past. He remembered the furious anger at being disturbed; he remembered the insults, the sarcasm, the rudeness, the impatience, the rage and the venom—and he sighed at the frailty of human nature.

But being basically and essentially fair-minded, he also remembereed that whenever he had asked for something, it had always been done, with swift and commendable efficiency. M. le Chef had often opposed him, criticized him, hampered him, obstructed him, frustrated him, thwarted him, reviled him, insulted him and even ridiculed him—but he had never let him down.

Perhaps all that vituperation and abuse had been part of a deliberate and calculated plan—perhaps after all these years of association M. le Chef knew so little of his character that he honestly imagined that this was the correct method of keeping him on his toes, the right way to inspire and goad him to even greater efforts, to work even harder . . .

It was a curious experience—something like watching a newsreel of his own life unfolding steadily in a backward direction—slowly in that his mind raced ahead to remember so much more at the same time—intense in its almost blinding clarity—and somehow pitifully sad.

If only people knew. Or if only they took the trouble to find out that behind and underneath every business relationship there was and must be a human contact, so much greater, so infinitely more important. How much more could he have achieved in his life with a little encouragement and occasional praise, instead of this eternal and senseless cracking of the whip he had always been compelled to endure. But it served no purpose to recall that now—the past was dead. And that was another thing he found somehow pitifully sad . . .

From the depths of his thoughts he became aware that Lorette was speaking again.

'I think this ambition—this urge to succeed at all costs and by his own unaided efforts—was all part of that almost pathological fear he had of growing old. He could not stand the thought of failure, in anything—he had to win, he had to drive himself and other people and he had to work harder than anyone else. All this was a compulsion which spurred and goaded him on and on. I watched it and could not stop it. I watched it and it frightened me, because I could not do anything. I could only think—how then would he contemplate the greatest failure of all, the one each and all of us must face in the end—the failure of fighting with old age and death?'

'That is the last battle no one wins," he said quietly.

'Yes. But this he would not accept. When he had to have false teeth, he brooded for weeks. He would not see or talk to anyone. He would not even go to the office, if you remember. When he had to have spectacles for reading, he spent hours by the window, holding a pencil out at arm's length and doing eye-exercises in the hope that he might be able to dispense with them. Something the oculist said about eye-muscles must have given him the hope. You know he does exercises every morning and takes a walk each evening to—'

'Yes—too many people seem to know about that.'

'I know. He boasts about it—to everyone. And yet, strangely enough, it was the sum of these very qualities—or rather, the attitude of mind responsible for them—that attracted me so strongly to him in the first place.

'Here was a man, brilliant at his profession, calm and confident and poised, with an authority and an intelligence that made him outstanding—with all the advantages and the experience of age, which made all my other acquaintances seem uncouth and callow—who refused to accept the idea of growing old, either physically or mentally.

'To a girl, young and inexperienced and smarting from a disastrous love affair, these qualities seemed to be entirely admirable and even splendid. Can you wonder that I fell in love with him on sight?'

She laughed, hardly and without mirth.

'And now I am describing them to you as pathological fears—how quickly the sweet savour of courtship becomes the harsh reality of marriage.'

'You must not get bitter—' he began gently.

The knee dropped, the foot slammed down hard and the dress flew up.

'Bitter?' she interrupted in a sudden and flaring rage. 'Of course I am bitter. You too would be bitter. I am also sick and tired and unhappy and frustrated and disillusioned. Tell me something honestly and truthfully, M'sieu Pinaud —do you think he killed her?'

He could only stare, with his mouth open, speechless with astonishment.

'Well—do you?'

'What on earth makes you say that?'

She changed her posture. This time she crossed her legs.

As she had not troubled to pull down her skirt and he was sitting opposite, M. Pinaud began to find a certain difficulty, not only in keeping his mind on the manifold problems of M. le Chef but also in curbing and controlling the inevitable physical effect of the excessive flights of his vivid imagination.

At the moment there was work to be done. Such thoughts, consequently, had to be controlled. And therefore, with a conscientiousness that was characteristic, he persisted, with single-minded and determined absorption, in surmounting the difficulty until his object was achieved.

She had not only changed her posture, but also her mood. The blood coursed to her brow as she began to speak.

But even in that second before she continued, M. Pinaud, being only human, considered several things at the same time with that incredible rapidity which is the wonder and the miracle of thought.

So there was work to be done. He was used to this, and would work competently and well for as long as was necessary—even harder than other men who were paid a greater salary—but in the end, however long and arduous, every day's work had some time to come to an end. And then it would be night. Then he could enjoy the ecstatic freedom of his imagination, soaring on wings of exultation. Then he would not even have to think about M. le Chef—since he would be asleep in Pontlieu gaol . . .

'Because it all seems to tie up with what I was telling you. This business of the housemaids has been going on for a long time—ever since he refused to come with me to visit the family. At first I was innocent and agreed. With complete trust it is so easy to be deceived.

'Marie Robinet comes in every day from the village to cook and clean, but we have no one living in the house.'

A spasm of pain crossed her features.

'Except when I go away. And Bayard is too old to get up early enough in the morning to make breakfast for Charles.'

She paused for a moment and her blush grew deeper.

'When I found out I was so furious I did not stop to think. I—I refused to sleep with him.'

'That was a mistake,' observed M. Pinaud quietly, his voice completely expressionless. 'All you did by that was to start a vicious circle. He is a passionate man.'

'I know. Who should know better?'

Her face now was almost scarlet. He could imagine her shame and mortification and admired her courage in going on.

'One makes the most appalling mistakes in marriage—'

'That is inevitable. Provided one learns from them and does not repeat them, the marriage can endure.'

'Not ours. But I learnt by this one. My only excuse—no, not excuse, but explanation—is that I was so humiliated I lost my temper and went almost mad with rage. I could not think clearly or rationally. Of course it was the worst thing I could have done to someone of his temperament.

'Now I realize that he was only trying to prove himself—his vigour—his virility—the very manhood he is so terrified of losing. What if something went wrong last night? What if he became impotent or something and blamed her? What if she jeered at him and ridiculed him? You know his temper. What if—'

'And yet,' he interrupted carefully and slowly, 'you were the one who insisted on calling the police.'

She met his eyes steadily.

'Of course. It was the only thing to do. He was in a panic—he could not even think clearly. He had some idea of burying the body in the garden and saying she had left unexpectedly—the first place they would have searched when she did not appear at her home. You know what village gossip can be like—everyone here knows about his housemaids.'

'Why are you telling me all this?' he asked quietly.

'Because if he did it he must be punished. If he is innocent, then you and Maître Mansard will prove it and there will be no more gossip.'

For a long moment there was silence. It could be as simple as that, M. Pinaud thought, but he doubted if it was.

* * *

The silence seemed to grow and enfold them in soothing and shrouding waves, sweeping down from the shadows of that vast and tranquil room in which they were sitting, and surging softly backwards from the thoughts in the innermost recesses of their minds.

Thinking of all that she had told him, he felt very close to her. Pity and compassion seemed to give a greater understanding, a deeper insight. He wanted to help her, but did not know how.

'So you see,' she said suddenly, 'your reasons for bringing me back here were hardly valid if you—'

'Of course they were valid,' he interrupted quickly, speaking with great intensity. 'I told you he needed you and I told you not to run away from trouble but to face it.'

The other reason—being always completely honest with himself—he was bound to admit and accept, but having done so he put it sternly from his mind.

She looked at him curiously.

'Then—all that I have told you—about the failure of our marriage—has made no difference—'

'None at all.'

He smiled suddenly as he spoke and his hard and strong features were transfigured.

'Marriage is a holy thing, Lorette, and therefore is given the strength to endure far worse things—'

'There can't be many worse.'

The smile vanished and his expression grew sombre.

'That is what you think. You are mercifully still young. He still needs you, more than ever now.'

'But why—'

'Because his whole life has been uprooted. Everything he believed in—his importance, his authority, the position of eminence he has worked so hard to achieve—has collapsed and crumbled in ruins. Even his self-respect—can you imagine what it means to him—to be locked up in gaol like a criminal—'

'He may be one.'

'Never. Nonsense. That I refuse to believe.'

Again she looked at him with a curiosity so intense as to be almost wonder.

'You really mean that, don't you? You have no doubts— no fears—no hesitations. He said you were loyal—'

'It is not a matter of loyalty. He gave me his word.'

She smiled with a haunting sadness.

'What else is that but loyalty? How often did he give me his word and break it? What about the word he gave in the church, in front of the priest and in the presence of God? You are the one who is still mercifully young, M'sieu Pinaud. You have kept your illusions.'

There was an answer to that and he opened his mouth to give it, but she did not pause.

'Perhaps he needed a lesson. It seems to be a hard one, but those are the only kind which count. This is the only one he will understand. But you are wrong—he does not need me. That has been the trouble. He has never needed me.'

'He does now.'

His voice was quiet and final and utterly convinced.

There was another silence. Then, suddenly, she seemed to make up her mind.

'Very well. What are you going to do?'

'I am going to see Henri Bayard and then M'sieu Poidevin. They may have noticed something.'

He had also decided to see her uncle again, but this he did not tell her.

She glanced at her watch. He had not noticed before that there was no clock in the room.

'Do you realize it is after two? You must be starving.'

'I had not thought about food,' he said truthfully.

'Nonsense. I have heard all about your appetite. Marie came in this morning and I asked her to prepare something for you—if you don't mind having it in the kitchen—'

'Not at all. And you—'

'I am going to bed—to catch up on my sleep.'

He looked at her with compassion and understanding. She was so young and so spoiled and so wilful—and so incredibly lovely and desirable. His voice was gentle as he replied.

'Yes, that is the best thing. When you have rested—go to see him. Make the first move yourself—it is always the hardest, because of your pride. Then you will see how much he needs you.'

There was a chicken-pie, which was delicious. It was also small, and so he finished it.

There was a dish, consisting of half-a-dozen hard-boiled eggs protruding from a potato-salad, temptingly garnished with chopped parsley and cayenne pepper. This was large, so he contented himself with tactfully leaving a modest quarter, in case Lorette should be hungry when she woke up.

There was a cold haunch of ham, whose slices curled up wafer-thin under his skill with the razor-sharp carving knife, literally pleading to be eaten. It seemed a shame to disappoint them, so he ate what he had carved and then carved some more, since it was the most appetizing ham he had encountered for a long time.

Then he discovered the soup in a large saucepan on the cooker. He switched on the hot-plate underneath. He was inordinately fond of soup, and after tasting it with a spoon came to the conclusion that this Marie Robinet was in her own right an artist.

Perhaps the bottle of Neuchâtel which he had found already chilled in the refrigerator and whose slightly acrid and yet delightful *bouquet* had done so much to enhance the flavour of the pie and the egg-salad, and the bottle of Hermitage already on the table—which no doubt had interpreted what the slices of ham had been saying—perhaps the combined effects of both helped to induce a certain tolerance, even contempt, for the rigid and established conventions of eating.

The fact that he had only just become aware of the soup in no way affected his determination to finish it. The fact that it was customary to begin and not end a meal with soup in no way altered his decision. The fact that his tasting had confirmed that this was a soup in a thousand, the triumph of a supreme artist, only increased his impatience and created and whetted within him a new appetite.

It was a pity that electricity, with all its advantages, was so slow. With gas he would have already been eating by now.

There were also two long loaves, baked early that morning in the village oven, fresh Normandy butter, and a noble cheese something like a small cart-wheel, whose exquisite flavour made of its dimensions initially a challenge, later a mockery and finally a humiliation . . .

He contemplated what was left on the table with resignation. If Lorette were really hungry when she came down, she could make a very satisfactory meal with the remainder of the egg-salad and such a noble cheese. She would have to buy more bread, of course, he reflected as he put the last piece of crust thoughtfully into his mouth. Perhaps he ought to call in at the baker on his way back and bring another loaf with him.

He wondered who could have told Lorette about his appetite. Probably M. le Chef. It was astonishing how rumour always distorted and exaggerated the most normal of human characteristics. . . .

7

Henri Bayard was old, but still tall and lean and active. With his deeply lined and craggy features and his massive balding head, which he held with the pride of a lion, he looked more like a retired general than an odd-job man.

He was holding the door open as M. Pinaud climbed the stairs from the side of the garage.

'Come in,' he said shortly. 'I saw you walking across the courtyard. You want to talk to me?'

'Yes,' replied M. Pinaud, just as shortly, but for a different reason. The stairs were steep and his lunch had hardly been a light snack.

The one large room was beautifully proportioned, but almost monastic in the severe austerity of its furnishing.

An iron bedstead stood in one corner, a plain table and two wooden chairs in another, a small wardrobe in a third. On the table in a black ebony and silver frame, stood a photograph of the head of a very lovely young girl. A crucifix of matching ebony and silver hung on the wall above it. The others were bare. The floor was of polished pine boards, with a single small runner carpet beside the bed.

'I am Pinaud,' he began, 'from the—'

'I know who you are,' interrupted the old man calmly, 'and I also know why you are here. What do you want?'

M. Pinaud thought swiftly. Here was a pride and a fierce authority it would be hard to break. On the other hand, it might be induced to bend.

'Just a few questions, M'sieu Bayard,' he replied quietly, his voice expressionless, deliberately ignoring the hostility in the other man's tone, 'about last night. I understand you went out in the evening, some time between nine and ten?'

'Yes. I go out each evening.'

'It was still light?'

'Yes. At this time of the year it is still light.'

'Did you see anything unusual? Did you notice any person walking or waiting near the house?'

'No.'

'May I ask you where you went? Did you go to the village café. Can anyone confirm your statement?'

The fierce old eyes grew stern and sad at the same time.

'No, M'sieu Pinaud. I was alone. There is no one who can confirm my statement, except myself. I will show you where I went, if you are interested. I should not go and never have been to the village café. Man's body is a pure and holy vessel, made in God's own image, from which His holy spirit can be poured on those occasions which are so rare as to be blessed. It is therefore not to be defiled by drink or smoke, nor by incontinent lusts.'

There was a long silence. The sadness seemed to surge out from the old man's eyes to enfold him, even as his words, with all their beauty and all their truth, took wings as if of their own volition and flew to touch him with gentle and grieving hands, tender and poignant and infinitely compassionate . . .

Almost desperate with the unendurable tension of that moment, he gestured towards the photograph on the table. He did not have to speak. Bayard answered his unspoken question as soon as his hand moved.

'My grand-daughter, Yvonne. She is dead.'

'I am sorry.'

The old man looked at him strangely and then inclined his proud head in a gesture of courtesy and acknowledgment far more eloquent than any spoken words.

Then he seemed to make up his mind. He walked to the door and from a peg behind it took down an old and shapeless tweed hat, which he put on his head. Then he went to the wardrobe, opened the door, and took out a walking-stick with a massive silver head.

'If you have the time, M'sieu Pinaud,' he said quietly, 'and if you would care to come, I will show you where I went last night.'

They walked together across the park that surrounded the manor-house towards the village to where the small and ancient church thrust its slender spire against the sky from amidst a bower of tall and stately trees.

M. Pinaud was the first to break the silence.

'That is a most unusual walking-stick you have there, M'sieu Bayard,' he remarked.

The old man loosened his grip, jerked his arm upwards suddenly and caught the stick again around its shaft. The silver head glinted in the sunlight. It was in the form of a hexagonal cube, richly and ornately chased, and set not at the customary angle of a head, but in line with and as an extension of the shaft.

'Yes,' he replied slowly. 'The silver is extremely thick, but it is not solid. The core inside is of lead, to give it extra weight. It has been in the possession of my family for some three hundred years.'

'That is interesting. But why make extra weight to carry? Surely—'

'As a weapon, of course,' the old man interrupted calmly. 'I have no records of what the original owner did, but I know it was old when my ancestor bought it. And I do know for a fact of family history that quite a number of skulls were cracked with it during the Revolution.'

He thrust the stick almost under M. Pinaud's nose as they continued to walk towards the church.

'Look at the head—see how the sides of the hexagon are all dented and bruised. That is how it was when I inherited it from my father. I have never wished to have it repaired.'

He paused and laughed, hardly and fiercely—a single savage bark of sound that held in itself nothing of joy or mirth. Then he withdrew the stick and his large and still powerful hand closed over the head.

'Indeed—I added a few more dents myself, when I was in the Resistance. To carry weapons was forbidden and dangerous—too many searches—but who would suspect a walking-stick, too slim to be a sword-stick, with the head concealed like this beneath my hand?'

Again he uttered that short and almost indescribable sound. Unaccountably it now struck M. Pinaud as menacing.

'What sentry would suspect a man alone—a man in a

soutane and a broad-brimmed hat? I knew a few words of German, sufficient to hold his interest.

'The first blow—a sudden forward jab—was always on the bridge of the nose, smashing it and filling the throat with blood, so that he could not call out and choked if he tried. The second in the mouth for the same reason and to make sure with some broken teeth. I usually managed to catch his automatic rifle with the other hand, but by then my friends were beside me with their knives and grenades.'

'But—'

'In this world,' the old man interrupted him calmly, 'there is good and there is evil. They have always been in conflict and they have always fought, since the beginning of time. Men have given them different names, which has made no difference. I had no choice. My country was occupied, by a nation with the sickness of power and corruption in its veins. My country was being poisoned. We had to cut the poison out.'

'I know what you mean and I agree with you,' said M. Pinaud. 'And yet—'

Again the old man interrupted him, calmly and quietly and decisively.

'There are people in this country who have prayed and still pray for me. I have felt as a living inspiration the grace and the mercy of their prayers. I can live with what I have done.'

There was a long silence. Then Henri Bayard spoke again, quietly and with a great solemnity.

'They thought, because I was a man of God, that they had nothing to fear. By the time they found out their mistake it was too late. True enough, I was a man of God. But for that very reason I was also God's instrument. They that live by the sword shall perish by the sword.'

In the ensuing silence, in the warm clarity of a sunshine that limned the peaceful tree-studded parkland with a brush of gold, M. Pinaud suddenly shivered, as if with cold. His thoughts, vivid and frightening and confused, had raced at the old man's words and the horror of his imagining seemed to lay an icy hand on his heart.

As they reached the gate of the small cemetery within the churchyard Henri Bayard spoke again, as if there had been no silence after his last remark.

'And they that live with lust, M'sieu Pinaud, shall also perish in lust.'

Suddenly M. Pinaud understood—or thought he understood.

'You mean—' he began excitedly, and then checked himself. He was speaking to the empty air. The old man had opened the gate and was already inside the cemetery.

It was small and beautifully kept, the grass neatly clipped, the flints white and free from weeds, the trees pruned and no dead flowers visible in any vase.

Henri Bayard walked straight to a corner grave, took off his tweed hat and knelt down reverently beside the simple headstone.

M. Pinaud waited outside the gate. This was a privacy into which he would not intrude, a sanctuary he felt obliged to respect.

When the old man rejoined him there were tears in his eyes. He made no attempt to wipe them.

'This is where I was last night,' he said simply and quietly. 'This is where I come every evening, when my work is done, to pray beside the grave of my grand-daughter Yvonne. It is the best time to pray, when the day is over and done. One can ask forgiveness then for having wasted it.'

They began to walk back together across the park. The old man spoke again, his voice now gentle and ineffably tender.

'I remember her at her first communion. She wore a white dress, white stockings and black shoes. And white gloves. And her grandmother's lace veil around her head. She looked a picture, everyone said. To me she looked like an angel.'

For a while there was silence. Then M. Pinaud chose his words with care.

'Just before you went in the gate, M'sieu Bayard,' he

said, 'you mentioned something which interested me, about those who live with lust—'

'What of it?' the old man interrupted.

'I presume you were referring to your employer.'

'You mean my late employer.'

'As you wish'.

'Yes, I was.'

He hesitated for a moment. M. Pinaud waited.

'Do you wish me to speak plainly? Do you want the truth?'

'Of course.'

'But you will not like it. You are here on his behalf.'

'He is also my employer. And he is my friend.'

'Then I pity you. In the same way that I pity his young wife.'

'Why?'

'Because he should be no man's friend. He is a fornicator, a copulator, a man attached to his sexual organ. He deserved to be punished. He is now in gaol, where he belongs.'

He did not raise his voice as he said this, which somehow seemed to give the words extraordinary intensity.

'Then why,' said M. Pinaud, 'if you feel like that—why did you come here to work for him?'

The deeply lined features were inscrutable, the fierce and hooded eyes as hard as agate. But there was no hesitation in the reply.

'Because Yvonne is buried here and I am the only one left of her family.'

M. Pinaud's voice was gentle.

'Tell me about her.'

The old man walked on for some time before he answered. His voice was slow and hesitant, almost as if he were expressing thoughts he himself found hard to remember.

'Yvonne was young—a mere child. Her parents were both killed in a car crash involving a motorcyclist. He was badly injured, but lived, and his wife brought an action against the estate for compensation and loss of earnings. They found two witnesses to swear that the accident had not been his fault. In consequence the insurance company denied responsibility. By the time the court expenses, the lawyers' fees and the damages had been paid, there was nothing left of the estate and she was a pauper.

'She faced the situation with courage, refused all my offers of help and determined to earn her own living. The family had lived in these parts and she heard that a house-maid was needed here. She applied for the situation, mean-ing to continue with her studies in the evenings to qualify for a better position. She was a good girl and prepared to work hard for the sake of the pride she took in her inde-pendence.'

He paused for a moment, and then when he continued there was no longer any hesitation in his voice, only anger and bitterness and a great and poignant sadness.

'And that swine corrupted and debauched her. He did not need a housemaid—he wanted a tart for his bed, like the one who got herself murdered last night. That was no housemaid—a whore from the slums behind the Gare du Nord, if ever I saw one.'

'How would you know that, M'sieu Bayard?'

'I was not always a man of God, I should tell you—nor am I ashamed to say it. But my grand-daughter, M'sieu Pinaud, was young and sensitive and a virgin. She felt ashamed enough to commit suicide.'

By now they had crossed the park and reached the court-yard of the manor-house. They stood facing each other in the bright strong sunshine.

'I am sorry,' said M. Pinaud, for the second time, mak-ing no attempt to conceal the shock, the surprise and the disgust from his voice. 'I did not know that.'

'Of course not. No one knew. It was successfully hushed up. With money and influence these days anything can be hushed up—even the murder of an innocent young girl. She left no note. The verdict at the inquest was suicide whilst of unsound mind. Unsound mind—nonsense. Her mind was brilliantly sane—as sound as yours or mine. I know what was wrong with her mind at that moment—it was frightened and bewildered—shocked and hurt beyond all endurance.'

There was a long silence. When M. Pinaud spoke his voice was strangely hesitant.

'You said murder, M'sieu Bayard. Isn't that rather a strong—'

'Of course it was murder,' the old man interrupted him with a sudden and blazing anger. 'He did not take a knife and cut her throat—but it was murder, just the same. That is why I used the word. That swine murdered her as surely as if he had shot her or bashed her head in. Morally he murdered her. He drove her to kill herself—isn't that murder?'

'There was no note. We do not know—'

He still hesitated as he spoke, sick at heart and unable to believe in what he had heard. And again the old man interrupted him.

'We do not have to know. I do not need to know anything when I have the evidence of a dead body and the headstone of a grave in front of me. And look at him now, M'sieu Pinaud—where have his sins taken him now? Vengeance is mine, saith the Lord, I will repay.'

He quoted resonantly with the authority and the familiarity of a man of God, M. Pinaud reflected sombrely. And for that very reason he considered himself to be the instrument of God. To what lengths could such a belief and the strength of such a conviction have driven him?

For a long time he stood there in the bright hot light of the sun, thinking. What should he do now?

There was no need to check on the old man's story, even had it been possible to do so. Either he believed it or he did not.

If he believed it he would have to speak to M. le Chef, the sooner the better. But that was a personal problem, which concerned him only, and had nothing to do with the case.

If he did not believe it, then the matter immediately became rather more complicated. If he did not accept what he had been told, then there was only one thing to be done.

He could either ask permission to borrow the walking-stick or simply take it without the owner's knowledge. In the same way that he could ask for the tyre-lever on the floor of the Ferrari or open the door—the car was unlocked—and take it. The owner of the pokers and tongs in the hall of the manor-house was not in a position to argue or dispute his actions—he could take them all as well.

In the forensic laboratory at Paris they had equipment sensitive enough to distinguish blood traces on newly sterilized surgical instruments. Even if the whole of his collection had been washed, the evidence would still be there.

Then he would have the weapon. But he still would not know who had used it. Except in the case of the walking-stick, which the old man obviously carried with him wherever he went.

He decided that this was something he would do, at the earliest opportunity.

8

'Am I to understand, M'sieu Pinaud,' the Duke asked slowly, 'that you are accusing my niece?'

His voice was quiet and cold and hard. M. Pinaud met his stare frankly.

'I am not accusing anyone,' he replied, his own voice carefully expressionless. 'But you must understand, M'sieu le Duc, that at this stage I suspect everyone. That is why I am here. I asked you this morning what time your niece left this house last night to go home. Your answer was vague—in the circumstances perhaps a little too vague. I have therefore asked you for the same information once again, to give you the chance to be a little more precise and definite. Does that answer your question?'

For a long moment their stares locked and held, the one arrogant and indigant, the other cool and dark and watchful.

Then the Duke sighed and seemed to come to a decision.

'I have never told lies in my life,' he said deliberately. 'I have been fortunate, naturally, in that I have never needed to. And therefore I do not intend to start now. She left almost immediately after dinner, as soon as we had finished our coffee.'

Having said this, his manner altered perceptibly, as if he had reached another decision. He pressed the bell on his desk.

M. Pinaud had not spoken. He sat in the chair opposite, his eyes dark with thought. When Jules knocked and opened the door he did not move or even look up.

'Have you eaten, M'sieu Pinaud?' asked the Duke. He was now once more the perfect host, calm and assured and urbane.

With a great effort M. Pinaud roused himself.

'I beg your pardon—yes, thank you. I had lunch.'

'Then I would suggest a little brandy for the digestion.'

'Thank you, M'sieu le Duc.'

'The decanter we had last night, Jules. It was excellent.'

'Very good, M'sieu le Duc.'

Jules bowed and withdrew.

The Duke waited, controlling his impatience with an effort. But M. Pinaud did not speak. He deliberately allowed the silence to swell between them, heavy and uneasy with the implications of all that had not been said. His patience was the greater.

'Well, M'sieu Pinaud—what are you thinking?'

He looked across the desk sombrely.

'I do not like my thoughts, M'sieu le Duc,' he replied quietly.

Jules knocked on the door and came in with the brandy, which he poured generously. Then he bowed himself out, allowing only the rigid lines of his back to express his unspoken disapproval.

They raised their glasses in silent salutation and drank, M. Pinaud with the utmost approval and satisfaction. The brandy was more than excellent. It was magnificent.

The Duke set his glass down carefully on the desk.

'She could have done it, I suppose,' he said quietly. 'God knows she had sufficient provocation, poor child. There is a wild streak in our family, you know, which has appeared periodically throughout the generations. And a woman scorned is an unpredictable creature. The insult to her womanhood and to her pride must have been intolerable—to find a housemaid in her own bed.'

He paused and drank again, and then replenished M. Pinaud's glass, which he saw was empty.

'I am trying to forget that she is my niece,' he continued slowly. 'I am trying to see this thing through your eyes, which is the only way to look at it. And yet even so—even though I said she could have done it—I do not believe for one moment that she did. I hope and pray that she did not. If she did, I will face the situation.'

'And get Maître Mansard again?'

That was an unworthy remark, and he felt ashamed as soon as he had said it. Perhaps it was the brandy that had spoken, and not him.

But the Duke only replied to the question as if he had been expecting it.

'Of course. No jury in the country would convict her. You know our attitude as a nation towards a *crime passionelle*— this would be classic.'

'Yes. But she is not on trial, M'sieu le Duc. No one is accusing her. At this stage I am only checking on the various facts. If she had driven that car of hers the way it was designed and built to be driven, she could easily have arrived in Pontlieu while her husband was out for his evening walk.'

'But she never drives it fast. She is terrified of it.'

'Then why did she buy it?'

'She didn't. I bought it for her as a birthday present.'

'Why that one?'

'Because she liked the look of it—and the colour, I suppose. In the same way that a woman buys a watch—if the case and the dial please her, that is enough. She does not want to know or cares what is inside. Have another brandy, M'sieu Pinaud.'

His glass had been replenished before he could express his thanks. He drank a little, this time more slowly, and thought how nice it would be if he could have a short sleep every afternoon, in the way that so many great and notable men had invariably made a habit of doing. The beneficial effects of such a practice were not and never had been the subject of any controversy. It did not need its exponents to extol its merits. No one but an idiot would attempt to deny what was so convincingly proved by their deeds and their fame.

Only, he reflected somewhat wistfully, the opportunity would be a fine thing. On this particular afternoon there was work to be done. There was always work to be done, on every afternoon—five days a week for M. le Chef and two days a week in his flat on permanent fatigues, to bring a light of appreciation to his wife's eyes.

And in spite of all the years of hard work he was neither great nor notable.

His exploits and his fame were certainly attracting an

increasing amount of attention, but slowly—far too slowly.
Using the most conservative ratio of time and proportional
increase, he calculated swiftly that he would be approxi-
mately one hundred and sixty-eight years old before he
could afford to do as he liked . . .

Depressed—not unnaturally—by these pessimistic
thoughts and conclusions, he fortified and comforted himself with some more of that magnificent brandy.

He suddenly became aware that the Duke was speaking.

'Lorette telephoned and told me that you had persuaded
Charles to stay where he is—in gaol. In view of all Maître
Mansard's efforts, may I say that this appears to me to be
ridiculous.'

'Not ridiculous,' he replied calmly, 'but necessary. Necessary and essential. Your efforts, M'sieu le Duc, and those
of Maître Mansard were not wasted. I was able to speak
to him, which was the most important thing of all. To hear
from his own lips what actually happened last night. But
in my opinion it would not be safe for him to leave that
gaol.'

The Duke's stare was both challenging and penetrating.

'If that is your opinion, M'sieu Pinaud, then obviously,
in view of your knowledge and experience, I have no
alternative but to accept it. But are you quite sure that no
other considerations have helped you to form it?'

There was a long silence. Because he was and always
had been completely honest with himself, M. Pinaud felt
the blood surge to his brow. He looked at his glass. This
was an occasion when a drink would have helped. But his
glass was empty.

'Your opinion is one single thing,' the quiet voice continued. 'The opinions of others are many and therefore
carry more weight. She is young and vulnerable, and she
has been very badly hurt. It would be neither fair not correct for both of you to be sleeping alone under the same
roof. People will talk. People are bound to talk.'

And the defendant in a *crime passionelle,* thought M.
Pinaud swiftly and a little bitterly, must always be completely above reproach. How otherwise could there be such
unanimous exoneration?

But he did not say this aloud. There was enough trouble already in this family without him adding to it.

'You are welcome, M'sieu Pinaud, to stay here, if you wish. We have ample room. But you would be rather far from the place of your investigations. I think the best thing would be to allow him out. Let him face whatever dangers there may be. They will perhaps make a man of him.'

He made up his mind quickly.

'Very well, M'sieu le Duc. I will get him out.'

'Good. Have another brandy before you go?'

He stood up.

'No thank you. It was excellent, but I still have work to do. Goodbye for now.'

He drove as far as the gravel path which had been laid across a field to link up the new house with the road, parked his car and walked to the front door.

The years had dealt kindly with M. Poidevin. He did not look any older. M. Pinaud found this vaguely irritating and at the same time a little sad, because for him the years had passed so quickly and were never the same . . .

But here were the same aristocratic and clean-cut features, the same appraising stare of deep-set and intelligent eyes, almost exactly as he remembered them from the past.

'How nice to see you once again, Pinaud. Do you remember when you came to ask me for a bottle of wine?'

Even the voice had not changed. Beneath its dry and husky inflection one could still discern the sardonic and mocking overtones. Here was a man who could contemplate the incomprehensible deviations of fate, the antics of his fellow-men and his own sins with resignation, amusement and tolerance.

'Of course, m'sieu. And you gave me a case of Montrachet.'

'So I did. What a memory. But what are we standing here for—come on in—come inside.'

The front room into which he had been ushered was new and yet tastefully designed in keeping with the age of the original barn. It was furnished with several choice pieces which M. Pinaud recognized from that gracious house in the Ile de France.

The chair he had cause to remember was still there, relegated to a corner. Slender and intricately carved and supremely uncomfortable, it might have suited the wizened and shrivelled buttocks of some sycophantic courtier in the days of Louis XV, but to him it had been like sitting on a plank.

M. Poidevin laughed softly.

'Yes. I see you remember. It is now for admiring only, since it is worth a fortune, but no longer for sitting. You looked like a bull balancing on a barge-pole—but you were too polite to complain. Take that one—you will find it more comfortable.'

'Thank you, m'sieu. I often wondered afterwards how the shape and configuration of the human posterior could have changed so drastically in a mere three hundred years.'

M. Poidevin laughed again and went to the sideboard. He opened a door and took out two glasses.

'If you would excuse me for a moment,' he said politely over his shoulder. 'I always keep some champagne in the refrigerator. At this time of day there is nothing better.'

He left the room and returned in a short while with a bottle beaded and frosted with moisture. He extracted the cork, poured the wine and filled the two glasses.

'Your good health, Pinaud.'

'And yours, m'sieu.'

The wine was very dry, cold and delicious.

'You are looking extremely fit and well, m'sieu,' M. Pinaud continued. 'If I do not presume—may I ask why you came to bury yourself in this remote corner of the world?'

'Because it was the most obvious and sensible and natural thing to do, Pinaud.'

He set a small table between them for their glasses and ashtrays, accepted a cigarette and sat down in an armchair.

'It is a long story,' he went on quietly, 'which I will try to make brief. You remember what you were up against when we met ten years ago—bribery and corruption and influence in high places?'

'Yes. I remember.'

'Well, if it was bad then, today it is a hundred times worse. In any large organization—and any group with authority and influence in these days must be large—you will always find a hard core of individuals whose only interest and ambition is to climb to the top, preferably by trampling on the necks of those thoughtless enough to get in their way. These people are utterly ruthless in their ambition and therefore will use any means available to achieve it—where could you find better material for infiltration?

'And always there are others—the small scum who stay at the bottom, who have neither the will nor the ambition to rise, who are always dissatisfied with their pay and therefore never too scrupulous as to how they augment it. Can you imagine the results that can be bought from these people with large sums of money?

'And those at the top? Why have they got to that position? It is a sad commentary on human nature, but usually it is because they want the money—the ultimate reward. Sometimes the power as well—but nearly always the money. Offer to double that money—tax-free—and how many will refuse or quibble about the conditions?

'The frightening thought is not only how far or how fast the poison has spread, but how little has been left untouched. Corruption is a creeping poison, like a virus in a bloodstream. Sooner or later the whole organism must be infected.

'There is so much money involved that the implications are terrifying. The smuggling of heroin on a large scale—one source of income—has become a well organized business with astronomical profits. You can imagine the value of one hundred kilos of pure heroin—this is just one case in a consignment. The old days of hiding a packet in the lining of a suitcase are out of date. It travels now in lorries with trailers and armed escorts to—'

'Armed escorts—surely not?'

M. Poidevin smiled. His smile was not sardonic but bitter.

'Yes. Armed escorts. This is big business. The power of

such money is unlimited. In Nice and Marseilles, as you have no doubt heard, they have already infiltrated into the police. They say every man has his price.'

He stood up, crossed over the room to the sideboard and came back with the bottle. He refilled their glasses and then stood there, the bottle still in his hand, looking down at M. Pinaud. Something that was almost but not quite a smile—a quivering of tenderness—touched briefly the corners of that mobile mouth.

'Not every man, Pinaud. Shall we say most men. You know the opinion I have always held of you.'

'Thank you, m'sieu, for the compliment.'

His voice was both sincere and grateful. M. Poidevin sat down, slowly and heavily. For one fleeting instant he seemed old.

'In Nice and Marseilles today—in Paris perhaps tomorrow. Who knows? The force of momentum and the power of success are already there, and the evil is spreading a little wider every month. Like a poison. Like I said.'

'Yes—we had heard rumours even in the *Sûreté* that—'

M. Poidevin held up one delicate and long-fingered hand.

'Of course. You must have heard. But please bear with me—allow me to finish, Pinaud, and then you can talk afterwards. I wanted to be brief, to answer your very natural question so that you can understand.

'I too, somewhat naturally, had heard all those rumours as well. And I heard more than rumours—I did not exactly sleep all day when I was Minister, I can assure you. I knew what was happening, and I could see very clearly what was going to happen in the very near future. And I did not like what I saw. I did not like it at all.

'I was almost due to retire. Suddenly I began to feel very old and tired. I do not know what actually prompted my decision, but one day I woke up and knew that it had been made. I decided to get out—to finish with the whole stinking mess of corruption—to resign. And perhaps to enjoy the last few years of my life in a manner that would bring me dignity and peace of mind, and a tranquillity and a satisfaction I no longer knew.

'I decided—although I am the first to realize now that

it was only the swing of the pendulum—to lead the simple life in the country. I would create a garden and grow flowers and chop wood. I would exchange the lies and the treachery and the double-dealing, the deceits and the trickery—for the fundamentals. I would listen to the birds in the morning and evening, watch sunrise and sunset, hear the wind in the trees and smell the new-cut grass—all the simple and lovely things I have never had time to do before.

'And perhaps, I thought—having lived a so-called civilized existence for nearly a lifetime—perhaps it would be an admirable contrast to die simple, having regained my sense of proportion and—more important—my sense of wonder, like a child. After all, there must always be a cycle in nature—we come into this life as children. Why not leave it like them, with wonder and acceptance and trust and—most essential of all—unafraid?'

There was a long silence.

M. Poidevin stood up, refilled their glasses and took the empty bottle out of the room, returning in a very short while with a full one. He sat down, accepted another of M. Pinaud's cigarettes and blew out a cloud of smoke.

'Does all that answer your question?' he asked quietly.

'Yes.'

Then M. Pinaud stirred restlessly in his chair.

'Didn't you think of fighting them?'

'Of course I did. I fought for years. I was fighting when I met you. You, a young and unknown detective, single-handed and without even the official backing of your chief, dared to question the authority of the strongest faction in the country. You were challenging vested interests and influences which had been predominant for centuries. I admired you for it. I had to help.'

Then he shook his head.

'But one gets so tired of being beaten, of being frustrated, let down, thwarted, obstructed and hindered. There is a sickness in seeing all one's efforts brought to nothing—over and over again. Making bricks without straw may be amusing as a recreation—but not as the work of a lifetime. There comes a day when it is easier not to get up when one knows the subsequent knocking down is inevitable.'

'I have had that all my life,' said M. Pinaud, quietly and with a simplicity that was somehow magnificent in its completely unconscious dignity. 'But I still get up.'

'Then I admire you. But you are younger. I think I must have grown old very suddenly.'

For a while they sat in silence, drinking the delicious cold wine, each one preoccupied with thought. Then M. Pinaud moved again in his chair.

'You know, of course, why I came to see you, m'sieu,' he said slowly.

'Yes. It must be about Charles. Otherwise you would not be here.'

'You heard what happened last night?'

'In a place like this we all know what happens almost as soon as it has taken place.'

'I came for the same reason I had many years ago—to ask you for your help.'

Again M. Poidevin shook his head.

'I am sorry, Pinaud. This time I cannot help you. I am no longer a Minister, but a private citizen.'

'It is just as that, m'sieu, you may be able to help me. I have all the official help I need.'

He stood up in one sudden movement and walked to the wide french-windows which took up nearly the whole of one wall.

A generous portion of the tree-studded parkland had been enclosed with fencing to make a large garden. At the far end a young man was shovelling a heap of top-soil. Beyond the lower fence, across the park and through the trees, the soft grey stone of the manor-house was visible, mellow and tranquil in the luminous evening light.

'Last night,' he said without turning round, 'between about nine and ten—did you see or notice anyone in the park? On the far side—near the manor-house?'

M. Poidevin came to join him at the window, carrying a full glass in each hand.

'No. Although I spent quite a time at this window,

watching and waiting for him to come. As he probably told you, I telephoned him and asked him to come over as soon as he could. I wanted to ask his advice about my garden.'

A sudden warm smile eradicated the sardonic and cynical lines about his mouth.

'Your imagination will tell you that when I have finished with it this is going to be a very beautiful garden. Trees and shrubs, lawns and flowers. I have managed to get a young fellow from the village to help me with the heavy work—you can see him there—but afterwards I shall look after it myself.'

The smile vanished and his voice, which had deepened with enthusiasm, changed.

'But Charles did not come. I expect he was too busy.'

He laughed shortly. The sound was light and mocking and sardonic.

'Village gossip has taken great care to keep me informed as to what went on in the manor-house. But as it is none of my business I was not very interested. I have invariably found that attempting to control one's own conduct leaves singularly little time for policing the morals of others.'

'Yes,' agreed M. Pinaud. 'While we are on the subject of morals, m'sieu—may I ask if you are living here alone?'

Again M. Poidevin laughed, this time with a little more genuine amusement.

'I am not entirely convinced that such a question is necessary, Pinaud. But no doubt you have some reason for asking it. The answer is yes. I live here and shall continue to live here alone. I am a confirmed bachelor. I thought you knew. I have been a bachelor since my wife died and my son got married.

'There are no problems. I manage very well. I have had years of practice. I eat a light breakfast and go out for lunch and dinner. There is a wonderful inn at Pontlieu—did you know?'

M. Pinaud shook his head abstractedly. He was looking out of the window and thinking of other things.

'I went there often in the past with Charles. That is one

of the main reasons why I decided to come here. The cooking is fantastic—something that has to be experienced to be believed.'

'I must try it then, m'sieu, as soon as I have time. This young fellow—you say he is local?'

'Yes.'

'What is his name?'

'Jean Lebrun.'

'Do you know what time he left last night?'

'He has been going home about six o'clock—but then he starts very early in the morning. I presume he left last night at the usual time. I got back here about eight o'clock —after my dinner at the inn—and he had gone.

'Because of this village gossip, I thought it tactful not to call in at the manor-house, but to wait here until Charles decided to come.'

He paused and gave a wry smile.

'Poor Charles. Perhaps it would have been better if I had gone to see him and insisted on the relatively greater importance of my garden compared with that of his copulation. It might have changed everything. But then—it is always easy to be wise after the event.'

'Yes, indeed, m'sieu. That was something you could not be expected to know. To come back to this gardener of yours—have you got his address?'

'Of course. He lives in the cottage beside the garage— number twenty-eight, I believe. But surely, Pinaud, you do not think—'

'At this stage, m'sieu, I think nothing,' he interrupted quickly. 'But I am interested in everybody who was in the vicinity of the manor-house yesterday evening. I will have a word with him on the way out.'

'Of course. Do that. He is not very bright, you will find, but a good worker.'

They went back to the chairs by the table, where M. Poidevin busied himself with the bottle.

'Tell me, Pinaud,' he said. 'What is happening about Charles?'

'He is in gaol. Inspector Salvan arrested him on suspicion of murder.'

'I know that. I was told the news this morning. I went to see him at once but I could not get past the Inspector. I suppose he is within his rights, according to the evidence, but what a way to handle things—after all, Charles is the head of the Paris *Sûreté*. You said you did not need official help—'

He paused and left the words a question.

'No, m'sieu. Inspector Salvan would not let me see him either, so I went to his uncle-in-law, the Duke. He telephoned Maître Mansard in Paris, used his influence and fixed things up on a really high level. Bail has been arranged and he will be out tonight.'

'Good. I heard the police-car late last night—the siren woke me up—but I assumed it was one of those official visits the inspector delights in. He hates Charles but does not hesitate to ask his advice.'

There was silence for a moment. Then M. Pinaud stood up.

'If you will excuse me, m'sieu,' he said politely, 'I will not keep you any longer. Thank you for your hospitality.'

'Not at all. It was good to see you again, Pinaud.'

'Thank you, m'sieu. I will have a word now with Jean Lebrun, if I may.'

'Of course. Come out through the french-windows here. There is a gate in the lower fence—hullo—he has gone. You must have just missed him.'

'Would he go through the park? Surely that is private land—'

'He might if he was in a hurry. No one here takes any notice of things like that. It is the quickest way to the village.'

'Then I will go that way. I might catch him up. If not, I can see him later at home. I left my car in the road, but I can collect that later.'

'All right. Keep in touch, Pinaud. I will see Charles tonight.'

9

As he came through the gate in the fence, he saw Lorette
walking across the park towards him.

He hastened to meet her, lengthening his stride with a
joyous anticipation. Her dress was now of a slightly darker
shade of blue, with a white collar and cuffs, the linen cool
and crisp and immaculately starched. He thought as she
came nearer that she looked even younger, even more
defenceless, even more desirable.

She smiled and called out long before he reached her.

'You said you were going to M'sieu Poidevin. I thought
it was about time you were due back.'

'You were right. And you timed it well. How are you
feeling? Did you have a good rest?'

'Yes, thank you. Although I did not sleep for long. I
have just been to see Charles. He wants to come out. He
says he does not mind the risks. He would sooner take
them rather than stay there any longer.'

The light from the evening sun picked out threads like
spun gold from her hair. The blue eyes looked at him
anxiously, and yet with complete trust and confidence.

He sighed and accepted the inevitable.

'Of course,' he replied quietly. 'That is not surprising. I
will go to fetch him.'

From behind the shelter of a thick laurel bush near them
a young man suddenly stepped into view. He wore heavy
boots, dirty jeans and an even dirtier T-shirt. He took a
couple of slouching steps nearer and then stopped.

'You won't be going anywhere to fetch anybody,' he
said in a rough and threatening voice.

He had a shock of long and unkempt hair and his eyes
were cold and flat, like those of a snake.

M. Pinaud looked at Lorette. She was staring behind
him with a wild fear in her eyes.

He half turned. A second youth was standing beside the

trunk of a tall and ancient poplar-tree, almost directly behind him.

This one had a low forehead and a bestial face. His hair was cropped so short it appeared almost white. He was short and burly and wore only a pair of black trousers. Almost his entire torso, thick-set and muscular, and even his shoulders and upper arms, were covered with a thick pelt of black hair.

His small and deep-set eyes were staring beyond M. Pinaud, and the light in their simian depths was ugly and unmistakable. One powerful hand was already fumbling at his belt-buckle.

M. Pinaud knew that there was going to be trouble. These two were tough and violent and bent on mischief.

The senseless savagery of violence—the mindless hate of the moron who has to destroy what he cannot understand— emanated from them both in every word and gesture with a menace that was sick and evil and almost physical in its intensity.

He reflected bitterly that if he had used his eyes normally as he walked—instead of keeping them glued on another man's wife—he would probably have noticed them as they changed their cover, long before they were able to come so close.

His voice as he spoke was cold and hard.

'You are trespassing, both of you. This is private land.'

'So what?' jeered the long-haired one. 'That's not all we are going to do—you can bet on that.'

Then he called to his mate.

'Don't be so impatient, you clot. Leave that belt alone for a bit. We've got something to do before we start stuffing her. Got to get him out of the way.'

In a second M. Pinaud's jacket was off and his gun in his hand. He stepped back quickly and swung the barrel from one to the other.

The vividness of his imagination brought terror and horror to his mind. Yet as he half turned to Lorette and whispered to her, nothing of his thoughts or his fears showed in his eyes, which were calm and cool and compelling. His voice too, was warm and rich with sympathy and encouragement. Her fear was as palpable as a physical thing and as such he had to fight it, before she gave up or broke down.

'Don't worry,' he whispered rapidly. 'You are lighter and faster than this one, and the other has heavy boots. Kick off your shoes, pull your skirt up to your waist and run like mad to your car. Get the police here as fast as you can.'

He took another two steps backwards to narrow his arc of fire and then suddenly roared in a parade-ground voice of command:

'Now, Lorette. Quick—now.'

One second each for the shoes and two seconds for the skirt, and then the rage and hate in the two men's eyes told him she must have gone like a startled fawn.

He did not dare take his eyes from them, and therefore it is perhaps regrettable but none the less understandable to relate (since his chronicler is concerned only with the truth) that as he aimed the gun carefully and deliberately and without compunction shot the hairy one in the foot, his only emotion was one of regret that he had not been able to watch her go . . .

And then—unexpectedly and paralysingly—he felt with sickening violence a sudden blow on his forearm. The muscles and tendons were numbed, and in an involuntary and reflex action, he dropped the gun.

A third youth had crept up behind him and now stood leering with a hammer in his hand. He too wore a dirty shirt, jeans and heavy boots, and his hair was even longer. His grin, as he bared ugly and discoloured teeth, was one of pure satisfaction. He balanced the hammer easily in his powerful hand.

'Next time a little harder—just on the same place,' he said softly. 'That will teach you to pull a gun on us.'

In that first instant of paralysing shock, their leader had moved with the speed of a striking snake, scooping up the gun in one swift and fluid motion.

Then he stepped back, slid out the magazine and tossed the gun into a bush.

'You won't need this now mate,' he said roughly.

The hairy one with the bullet in his foot had not spoken or moved, except to lean against the tree-trunk for support. A knife had appeared in his hand, and his eyes never left M. Pinaud's face. The other one stood quite close, idly shifting his grip on the hammer.

M. Pinaud stood there tensely, fighting the waves of nausea from the agony in his arm.

The parkland no longer seemed beautiful in the tranquil evening light, but dark and menacing and unfamiliar with fear—a sombre backdrop for all the suppressed savagery and violence which inevitably was about to explode.

The leader pressed the spring catch and began to extract the shells from the magazine, flipping them over his shoulder one by one.

'She loves me. She loves me not. She loves me. She loves me not. I can soon make her love me. We can all make her love me.'

He tossed the empty magazine after the shells and his voice changed.

'That was a dirty trick—to make her run away like that. And to shoot my mate in the foot. But you look like a filthy spoil-sport to me. You will have to be punished. My mates are good at punishing people like you. You would not believe what damage a pen-knife and a hammer can do, once a man's trousers are down.'

M. Pinaud did not answer. Every moment that passed gave Lorette a better chance and helped his arm to recover.

As if he read these thoughts the youth's voice changed again.

'When we have attended to you—then we will have to chase her. Women can't run, anyway. And even if she could—who would believe her, with her skirt up around her neck? Salvan will lock her up for indecent exposure as soon as he sees her.'

M. Pinaud fought the anger that surged up like a wave behind the mocking and defiling words—he fought his anger because it had no place and was of no use at this time, and concentrated instead on forcing the fingers of his hand to move and clench and extend and relax and move again and stiffen and close and open—again and again—ignoring that with each effort and muscular rhythm he had to endure an intensity of pain and agony from the bruised and perhaps even lacerated tendons in his forearm.

'You are all a long way from home, aren't you?' he asked, and his voice was cool and confident. It was also deliberately condescending and completely infuriating. 'Why don't you go back to crawl in the slums where you belong? You are out of place in the country here—where are your bicycle-chains and your razor-blades? And surely you have forgotten to bring enough of your friends—it usually takes six of your kind to hold a man down while you give him the boot.'

He had been jeering at their leader deliberately, hoping to provoke him, to goad him into making some mistake. It was his only hope—the odds were too great.

But it was the hairy one who cracked first. He had been leaning against the trunk of the great poplar-tree which had so successfully concealed him. His face was grey and glistening with sweat, and yet in spite of the pain he must have been suffering, he had not uttered a sound.

Now, at M. Pinaud's words, he gave a wild and almost inhuman cry of rage and forced himself upright with one hand away from the trunk, swaying uncertainly on his one sound foot. The other hand, grasping the knife, was held back, well behind him.

M. Pinaud saw his knees bend and knew that the time had come. He flung himself down on to his good hand and exploded into action.

The knife glittered in the sun like a wheel of light. It flashed a second later past the exact place where M. Pinaud's head had been.

The hairy one overbalanced with the effort of throwing, swayed and crashed down, a shriek of agony bursting from his throat as he wrenched his wounded foot.

The shriek mingled discordantly and simultaneously with

another yell of pain. Almost before he was horizontal, M. Pinaud's foot had lashed out in a deadly *savate* kick and his heavy boot smashed with accurate and paralysing force into the long-haired youth's knee-cap.

The hammer flew out of his hand as he fell to the ground.

Then, before M. Pinaud could get up, the leader had jumped on him with savage and sickening violence.

One heavy boot kicked his supporting hand away, the other smashed into his throbbing forearm to send waves of agony into his head that threatened to engulf his whole mind with blackness.

Desperately, instinctively, he fought to control his swimming senses and tried to roll clear of those viciously kicking boots.

He saved his eyes by jerking his head back in the nick of time. The iron toe-cap tore a furrow of skin from his forehead and suddenly the green and golden scene was red with the tinge of his own blood.

One kick he reflected with his sound arm and one he took in the ribs before his chance came and he caught an ankle with his left hand in a grip of steel.

Exerting all his great strength in one supreme effort, he jerked and twisted, and the youth yelled and came down like a falling tree. His head must have struck a stone or a projecting root, because he lay there where he had fallen limp and inert and completely unconscious.

On his knees M. Pinaud wiped the blood from his eyes. Slowly and wearily he forced himself to his feet.

The hairy one seemed to have fainted with pain, the other one was huddled in a foetal position hugging his knee, moaning and crying like a child.

Soft and muted by the towering trees, the sound of a police siren echoed vaguely in his throbbing head.

He felt that he wanted to lie down and rest, and perhaps sleep, so that he could forget the pain. But he forced himself to go on. There was so much to be done, so little time in which to do it.

He was unarmed. He should never be unarmed. Not for the extension and the amplification of his own ego, which

most men derived from having a gun in their hand—surely
he had just proved he did not need that—but for the fact
that he represented the law. And the law for the common
good must necessarily be greater than any one individual
and therefore had to be enforced.

So he kept on his feet, hurt and shaken and bleeding,
and forced himself deliberately to walk until he found his
gun beneath the bush into which it had been tossed.

Now you have your gun, Pinaud, he told himself, you
are bound to realize that it is useless without any bullets.
Your spare clips are in the car and so will not be of much
use.

Therefore you had better extract your digit and banish
all these stupid thoughts you may have had about lying
down or resting or sleeping—and get on with the job and
find the magazine and the shells before you need to use
them. You know where he stood. You remember what he
did. You were watching him all the time. You saw where
he threw the gun. The shells and the clip he tossed over his
shoulder.

Come on, Pinaud—make an effort. There is no difficulty
in this task—if only it were not for the sickness and the
faintness and the pain in your arm and the blood trickling
down into your eyes—all you have to do is to stand here
and then look back—back to where he threw them—well
then if there is no difficulty and it has got to be done why
not get on with it instead of indulging in all this Russian
type of introspection . . .

And this was how Lorette found him—swaying on his
feet and yet indomitable, rapidly weakening and yet re-
fusing to acknowledge it, muttering to himself in a cease-
less and sternly disapproving monotone, searching almost
blindly for shells in the undergrowth, gasping with the pain
to his injured ribs each time he straightened up again and
liberally spattered with his own blood from head to foot.

They had left the police car in the courtyard of the
manor-house and ran through the parkland, which was the
quickest way. They all ran, Inspector Salvan and his two

policemen and Lorette, but Lorette ran faster than any of the others.

She had found another pair of shoes in the house and her skirt was where it should have been, but she was still the first one to reach him.

And now as she spoke all her heart was in her voice.

'You are hurt—bleeding—oh, what have they done to you?'

He looked at her and tried to smile.

'Nothing much—nothing that won't get better. I am glad you made it—'

Inspector Salvan and his two policemen were now beside them, but they could have been in another world. For him, there was only one entity, one existence. There were no other people—only this girl and her beauty, and the concern and the gratitude in her eyes.

She bit her lip to stop its sudden quivering and interrupted him almost fiercely.

'Of course I made it. I had the easy part. You stayed—you did this for me—a stranger you did not even know—that is what I find so hard to believe or understand. But we can talk later. Right now you need a doctor and a hospital from the look of you.'

'Later—later,' he muttered vaguely and went on looking for his ammunition.

'What on earth are you trying to do—kill yourself? You are hurt—you are bleeding—'

The men came nearer and nearer and by the fact of forcing themselves into their own private world caused her, in some tragic and inexplicable and infinitely lonely way, to disappear and he no longer saw her.

He saw only the red tinge all over the sunlight as the blood ran down again from his forehead and the three hard faces, threatening and frightening, smeared with his own blood and mouthing words he could no longer understand—nearer and nearer and more and more terrifying as the earth seemed to sweep up, not in a green but a bloodstained wave, and he crashed down unconscious . . .

10

In M. Pinaud's undeniably complex nature—as his discerning public will by now have gathered—the idealist and the perfectionist held equal status with a host of others.

It is therefore not surprising to relate that when he regained consciousness he fully hoped and expected—perhaps because of the memory of Lorette's last words—that he would find himself in a hospital under the skilled and vigilant care of doctors and nurses.

Throughout his life, thanks to a certain propensity for trouble which seemed to increase and not diminish with the years, he had been no stranger to hospitals.

He had always derived a particular sense of satisfaction—perhaps owing to the soothing helplessness engendered by his various injuries—from their hygenic cleanliness, their efficiency and above all from their impersonality.

His whole life, it sometimes seemed, had been a clash of personalities—the following of a lonely and terrifying path desecrated with the consequences of the outrageous misdeeds of human natures that were warped and twisted and depraved and sick.

It made a refreshing change, if only for a short time, to be treated not as a human being but as a case, as a chart, as a graph, as the confirmation of a diagnosis—to lie between clean sheets on a steel and sterile bed, to swallow pills and powders and capsules and watch bandages being changed and to eat plain and wholesome food and not drink or smoke for a change, and to study the individual features of the nursing Sisters of Mercy, each one framed in its coif of snow-white linen and to speculate—quite fruitlessly and unavailingly and yet with never failing fascination—as to what each one's life had been once upon a time and how much each one had renounced so long ago . . .

He knew that he was now conscious and aware. But he lay there, wherever he was, at full length, motionless for a long time with his eyes closed, feeling thankfully, with each passing moment of awareness, the strength and vitality stealing back, in a comforting and vital surge, into his body.

There was no sound, which was strange. One would normally have heard, even dimly and remotely, voices and noises from the other occupants of the ward. But there was no sound. Perhaps he was in a private ward, thanks to the influence and the generosity of Lorette's omnipotent uncle.

But even as the thought came—comforting and exciting in the unlimited possibilities of its implications—so he dismissed it as obviously wrong. The smell was wrong. This, all about him, was not a hospital smell.

He opened his eyes.

A naked and feeble light bulb was sunk in the far corner of a whitewashed ceiling. The one small window was high up, closed and barred. It was dark outside.

He lay on a narrow plank bed, covered by a single blanket. He wore the same shirt and trousers in which he had fought in the park. They were filthy and torn, reeking of stale perspiration and stiff with coagulated blood. His gun and shoulder-holster were missing and his jacket hung over the back of the single chair.

The door was thick and massive, with a narrow grating inset at eye-level from which one could see the bed. In the far corner stood an open toilet, from which the smell emanated. It was of human excrement.

It was not a hospital ward, nor yet a private room, but a cell. He was in Pontlieu's gaol.

He kept his eyes open then, because that way it was easier not to think, and just then he did not feel like thinking. He was too disgusted, too sick, too worried and—as he was the first to admit—too frightened. The implications of what had happened were terrifying.

And now that he was conscious, his head, his ribs and his arm had all begun to hurt again.

After some little while, he heard footsteps outside. The door was unlocked, unbolted and unbarred and a man came inside the cell, followed by a policeman wheeling a trolley.

The man was short and rotund and cheerful, with a bald head and twinkling and very shrewd eyes. He was dressed in a beautifully cut and obviously very expensive suit, which looked as though he slept in it by night and dribbled soup, egg and tobacco-ash down its front by day.

'Well—well, M'sieu Pinaud. Permit me to introduce myself. I am Joinville, the local doctor here. Inspector Salvan told me you needed a little attention when you arrived here.'

'That was kind of him—'

'No—no,' the doctor interrupted him cheerfully. 'It was obvious. Nothing to do with kindness at all. We have one corpse already here in Pontlieu—we don't want another one. I came here at once and have looked in at you several times. You were either asleep or unconscious—whichever it was I considered it the best thing for you.'

He paused for the briefest moment.

'So I decided to wait. I knew you would feel better when you woke up naturally, without any help from me. I was right. I am usually right. That is why I am a good doctor. That is why I act as police surgeon. You do feel better, don't you?' he concluded, with perhaps just the faintest trace of anxiety in his voice.

M. Pinaud smiled. He was such a cheerful little man. It would be a shame to disappoint him.

'Yes, Dr Joinville—definitely. And I shall feel even better when you have had a look at my ribs, this gash and my arm.'

'Of course—of course. That is why I am here.'

The policeman, who had been patiently waiting, now wheeled the trolley beside the bed and then went out, closing but not re-locking the door. On the trolley were several shallow bowls of hot water, various bottles, tubes and small boxes, lint, cotton-wool and bandages.

Dr Joinville went to the other side of the bed. First of all he unbuttoned M. Pinaud's shirt, pulled up his singlet, and then felt and probed and palped his ribs with strong and yet delicate hands.

'Breathe in deeply,' he said.

M. Pinaud breathed in. The hands still moved.

'Cough.'

M. Pinaud coughed.

'Again.'

The hands were never still, feeling, exploring, assessing and judging.

'Which hurt the most?'

'Both.'

'Breathe in again.'

'Cough again.'

All the time his hands moved.

'What was it—a boot?'

'Yes.'

'You were lucky. You must have moved just in time to make the kick glancing and not frontal. They are bruised, I should think, but not broken. The pain will pass. Shall I strap them for support?'

'No, thank you.'

The doctor stared in surprise.

'Why not? It will help.'

'I have been strapped before—it is too restricting. I will have it done later. As long as nothing is broken I can stand the pain. The gash and my arm are more important.'

'As you wish.'

He then walked round the bed to the trolley and washed and dried his hands carefully after pouring an antiseptic into one of the bowls. Then he set to work, using another bowl of clean water, on M. Pinaud's forehead. He worked skilfully, rapidly and well, with a smiling and inspiring competence. The gash was washed and cleansed and liberally coated with a very painful antiseptic.

'Not deep enough for stitches,' he announced cheerfully. 'Just enough to bleed and make a mess, especially if you were exerting yourself. A piece of lint and a plaster will be sufficient for it to heal—I take it you don't want a bandage?'

Again M. Pinaud smiled.

'No, thank you—no bandage. People might get sympathetic. That would never do.'

He did not wait for the doctor's reaction, but held out his arm.

'This worried me far more. He used a hammer.'

Dr Joinville rolled up the shirt-sleeve and whistled softly at the sight of the huge yellow and purple bruise on M. Pinaud's forearm.

He probed and felt with skilful fingertips, iron-hard and delicate alternatively. With them, he encircled M. Pinaud's wrist and made him move and spread all his fingers, clench his fist and bend his elbow. He repeated all this performance with a magnifying glass stuck in one eye, by the light of a powerful torch which he asked M. Pinaud to hold in his other hand.

Then he straightened up, removed the glass, switched off the torch and smiled even more cheerfully.

'Again you were lucky,' he said quietly. 'Nothing broken. I would like to put a fairly tight bandage from wrist to elbow, for support—if you don't mind?'

M. Pinaud did not answer. Again that faint tinge of anxiety crept into the doctor's voice as he continued.

'It will help it to heal quickly—and the support will ease the pain. The shirt-sleeve will conceal—'

'I am sorry,' M. Pinaud interrupted quietly. 'I was thinking of something else. Please do whatever you think best.'

Thoughtfully he watched the firm and competent hands busy with the scissors and a roll of bandage. Then, when he spoke again, his voice was even quieter than before.

'Tell me, doctor—why am I in here?'

Dr Joinville did not stop what he was doing. He smeared ointment from a tube on to a square of lint which he placed over the bruise and then he began to wind on the bandage. Only as he worked M. Pinaud saw that all the light and laughter and all the twinkling cheerfulness had gone from his eyes. The shrewdness alone remained. His features suddenly looked old and tired and sad.

'I am sorry,' he replied in a flat and formal tone. 'I can't answer questions. I am paid to work for the police—that is all.'

The ointment was cool and soothing, the bandage exquisitely adjusted and masterfully wound—firm and supporting and yet not too constricting. His arm felt better already.

The doctor walked to the door and knocked. It was opened immediately. The policeman, who must have been waiting outside, came in and wheeled out the trolley. The doctor stood aside to allow him to pass. Then he turned to leave. He was obviously not going to say anything more.

'Thank you again, doctor,' said M. Pinaud, his voice carefully expressionless. 'For all you have done. And for your skill and competence. I feel very much better. Would you be kind enough to tell Inspector Salvan that I would like to see him.'

'Of course.'

Then he added over his shoulder, as if trying to reassure not only M. Pinaud but himself as well:

'I am paid to do a job. I try to do it well. That is all.'

The door closed behind him and was locked, bolted and barred.

Inspector Salvan's hot and restless eyes looked everywhere except at M. Pinaud, who was sitting up on the side of the plank bed.

'Of course I don't mind answering your question, M'sieu Pinaud. You have a perfect right to ask it. You are under arrest and will be held here in gaol until you have been formally charged.'

'Charged? With what?'

'Assault. Battery. Mayhem. Physical violence. Armed intimidation. Breach of peace with a deadly weapon. Manslaughter—if one of them dies.'

'Rot. Nonsense. There were three against me. They started it. I was defending myself. You must be mad.'

The inspector flushed slightly at his tone, but continued with his voice still even and controlled.

'We have five witnesses against your unsupported word. Two of the victims—one is still unconscious. The two policemen who were with me and myself.'

'Witnesses—those thugs?'

'They are not thugs, M'sieu Pinaud. They are perfectly respectable citizens, self-employed—'

'Then why did they attack me?'

'We have only your word that they attacked you.'

'Yes—my unsupported word. What about Madame Lorette? She saw and heard them. Didn't she tell you they were intending to rape her? Why did you come at all if you did not believe her?'

'Madame Lorette was in a hysterical state. She is a woman who has had a great deal of mental strain recently. Nevertheless, we had to investigate. That was my duty. We concluded that she saw you beating up these men, lost her head at your brutality and ran to fetch us. I have not seen her since and therefore have not been able to take her formal statement.'

M. Pinaud looked at him for a long time. Then he spoke, coldly and deliberately.

'Inspector Salvan, if I decide to ignore the nonsense you have just been telling me and accept the somewhat doubtful fact of your sanity—then I am faced immediately with only one alternative—the very nasty problem of your motives. Who is paying you to do this? Whose orders are you obeying?'

His tone was offensive, as he had meant it to be. The flush deepened under the inspector's sallow skin and a vein began to throb in the side of his forehead. His voice changed and became quick and venomous.

'What I am doing, M'sieu Pinaud, is none of your business. I am acting entirely within the bounds of my authority, and therefore do not have to justify my actions to you. You are, in our opinion, a dangerous criminal, and as such will remain locked up here where you belong and where you can do no more mischief until we decide what to do with you.'

'You mean until you get your new instructions.'

'Mind your own business. Perhaps this experience will teach you a lesson you badly need and richly deserve. You can't walk about this place assaulting respectable citizens—this isn't Paris, you know. You may get away with that sort of behaviour there, but not in Pontlieu.'

And he walked out, banging the door behind him.

* * *

M. Pinaud sat on the side of the bed, listening to the lock being turned, the bolts shot home and the bars descending.

He felt somehow that he was swimming in very deep waters.

He stood up, walked to the chair and felt in the pockets of his jacket. Strangely enough, a packet of cigarettes and his lighter were still there.

Thankfully, he lit a cigarette and went back to the bed. He was glad enough to lie on his back for a little while, smoking peacefully and trying to sort out his thoughts from the confusion in his mind.

Besides, the acrid blue smoke of his strong cigarettes helped to smother that appalling smell. It was a pity that he had forgotten to mention it to Inspector Salvan. It might have been the last straw on the camel's back—the final offensive jibe which might have made him lose his self-control completely and perhaps his discretion.

But the more he thought about the situation the more likely it seemed to him that the discretion of Inspector Salvan was of very little importance.

The mere fact that he had dared to arrest M. le Chef's best detective—after his recent salutary experience of both the Duke of Charanton's influence and Maître Mansard's competence—seemed to imply that he was only doing what he had been ordered and paid to do, very quickly, very urgently, very efficiently, and regardless of the consequences . . .

Which meant that to certain people M. Pinaud was becoming a nuisance. The attack in the park had obviously been planned to put him out of action. This had failed. That was why he was here in Pontlieu gaol—out of the way.

But why? Why was it so essential for him to be out of the way?

Because he was interfering with certain plans. Because he had arrived in Pontlieu unexpectedly, and as a result M. le Chef could now no longer be held a prisoner, but was free to go out on bail. He remembered what he had told Lorette in the park: I will go to fetch him. She had almost certainly passed this message on to Inspector Salvan, who would no longer dare to hold him after Maître Mansard's intervention.

Which meant that M. le Chef—taking his words to Lorette rightly as acceptance of his request to leave—had in all probability left with her. And was now at home, alone and defenceless. At home, vulnerable to people who did not stop at murder to get him out of the way. Out of the *Sûreté* and hence powerless to hinder their plans.

He remembered M. Poidevin's words, very vividly, very clearly, and with a terrifying sense of helplessness. The dice were loaded against him.

He threw the end of his still smoking cigarette on the stone floor and lit another one. To stamp it out he would have to get up. It was not worth the effort. Let it burn. Unfortunately, if would not set fire to the cell, but at least the extra smoke might help to counteract the smell.

The strong tobacco, as always, soothed and calmed his nerves. His head had ceased to throb and the bandage gave his arm a sense of strength and support.

Count your blessings, Pinaud, he told himself sternly. It could have been far worse. The dice are loaded. So what? They have always been loaded, all your life, ever since the old gods decided that heaven would be a dull place without laughter—just as they insist on expressing their somewhat macabre sense of humour by changing the game arbitrarily and dealing the cards themselves . . .

So why start to complain now? You have enjoyed all the games. It is how you played them that counts. To be allowed to participate is in itself the greatest of all privileges . . .

The door opened again and the sergeant came in.

'You have a visitor,' he said briefly. 'You are allowed ten minutes in the waiting-room. I have to remain outside to watch, but I do not listen.'

His manner was cool and informal, polite and completely disinterested.

'Good,' said M. Pinaud, his features expressionless. 'That is indeed a privilege.'

He got up from the bed and put on his jacket.

'Walk in front of me, please. Straight down the corridor. Second room on the left.'

'When do I eat?'

'The policeman will bring you a tray in about half an hour. In here, please.'

He closed the door, whose upper half was of clear glass, and stood outside.

And then there was nothing except the blue of her eyes and the gold of her hair in front of him and he saw nothing else. He could not have told you what the room was like. He did not care. He saw only the light in her eyes and heard in his heart all the things she felt but dared not say.

She caught her breath.

'Are you all right—your head?'

He smiled.

'Yes, thank you. They sent me a doctor. I am not a very prepossessing sight, I am afraid—'

'You did it for me. I shall never forget. What does it matter what you look like?'

'It is nice to feel clean. But never mind. Thank you for coming.'

'I am only sorry I did not come before. I went back with Charles—Inspector Salvan made no objection. And then we decided that the best thing to do to help you was to go at once to my uncle and ask him to get Maître Mansard again. But it is getting late—and this is the weekend. Nothing can be done until tomorrow—or even the next day.'

He thought about this and frowned in concentration.

'I am sorry—' she began anxiously.

'No—no—it is all right. I was only thinking. I am very grateful. But tomorrow may be too late—'

'What do you mean?'

'There are very strange things going on in this place. Your husband was safe while he was in here. That is why I advised him to stay. But he wanted to come out, you told me. Very well—that is his decision. But now he is out they may try again. They want him out of the way.'

'Who?'

'I don't know. There are certain people who want him out of the *Sûreté*—he is too honest to be corrupted. The pressure has been going on for a long time. Look, Lorette—would you please do something for me—'

'Of course.'

'Go back now. Go home as fast as you can. Lock up the house, front and back—doors, windows, shutters, everything—and wait for me. Don't open the door to anybody until I come. I will give a special ring—three quick and two slow.'

'But how can you—'

He smiled again.

'It will be simple. This is not a gaol, but a joke. Tell me—is Inspector Salvan here?'

'No. He usually goes home about six. He is on the telephone, of course, from his house.'

'What is the time now? My watch was smashed.'

'Just after eight.'

'How many policemen did you see in the building when you came in?'

'Two. One at the desk in the entrance and the sergeant who brought you here.'

'Yes. That would be normal.'

The sergeant opened the door.

'Time's up,' he said.

'Go now, Lorette. Remember what I told you.'

She stood up quickly.

'Promise me one thing,' she said quietly.

'Anything.'

'Take care of yourself. You have done so much for me.'

'I will. Goodbye for now.'

As he had told her, it was simple. Indeed, he reflected as he waited behind the door of his cell, it would have been strange and even humiliating if the greatest detective in the country could not get out of a tin-pot provincial gaol.

He waited patiently, without moving, listening attentively with every sense alert, until at last he heard the sound of footsteps. Then he moved away quickly from the door.

When it had been unlocked, unbolted and unbarred, the

policeman opened it, picked up the tray he had deposited on the floor outside and carried it in. Which was in every detail exactly what he had done a hundred times before with a hundred different prisoners. But which this time was a mistake. This prisoner was not like the hundred others.

M. Pinaud walked forward, slowly and naturally, from the side of the bed, his hands outstretched to take the tray.

The food looked quite appetizing. It would be a pity to waste it, especially as he was hungry. But he could not afford to wait, in case the procedure was to leave the empty tray in the cell until the morning.

'Thank you very much,' he said politely, and then jerked his knee up with sudden and savage violence into the man's stomach.

With one hand he managed to slide the tray on to the bed, so that the sound of smashing crockery through the open door would not bring the sergeant from his desk; with the other he caught the man's collar as he doubled up in agony and eased him to the floor.

In a few moments the policeman was effectively gagged with his handkerchief and M. Pinaud's tie, his ankles and wrists securely bound with his braces and belt.

The blanket was a mess of meat, potatoes and gravy. He rolled it up neatly and put the whole lot down quietly on the floor. Then he lifted the policeman on to the bed.

With the man's keys in his pocket and his gun ready in one hand he stepped into the corridor, closing but not locking the door behind him.

He walked quietly until he came to the desk at the entrance.

The sergeant looked up into the barrel of a very steady revolver, stiffened in every muscle for a second and then shrugged and relaxed. He had had enough experience to accept the inevitable.

'On your feet,' said M. Pinaud quietly. 'Your gun on the desk.'

He leant forward, snatched it up with his other hand and slipped it into his pocket.

'We are taking another walk. This time you will be in front of me. Back to my cell—quickly.'

The sergeant obeyed. He could tell from M. Pinaud's voice that he had no option.

'You will never get away with his,' he said over his shoulder.

M. Pinaud did not answer.

'In here,' he said when they reached his cell. The keys were ready in his other hand.

'Open the door—it is not locked. Right over to the other side.

He slammed the door shut and shot home one of the bolts as soon as the man was inside. Then he locked the door and set the bars in their sockets.

Then he ran back to the desk, relieved to find that the light was not glowing on the switchboard. With a penknife and a screwdriver he found in a drawer he disconnected the telephone.

He could not hope that this would be effective for long— when the police did not answer their telephone, whoever called, enquiries would be made, but it might give him a little more time for what he had to do.

11

The soft and mellowed stone of the manor-house seemed to swim beneath the moonlight, flooded with a sheen that had in it blue and grey and silver and an unearthly radiance that was all and none of these things at the same time.

In the moonlight it seemed to sleep, as it had slept in the peace and the tranquility of the ages, as it had slept in the sunshine, weathered and matured by the seasons, the wind and the rain, ageing and yet indestructible with the passing of time.

The house was shuttered and still. There was no need for the porch-light; the full moon rode proudly, high and bright and clear, through a cloudless sky.

He rang, three quick and two slow chimes, as they had agreed. Then he waited.

There was no sound, no sign of life. He rang again, with a vague feeling of apprehension stealing up like a coldness about his heart.

What could have gone wrong? Surely he had made himself clear. Surely she was intelligent enough to understand and to remember, even though women were notoriously vague about figures and numbers. Were they sitting there waiting for two quick and three slow chimes?

He was about to ring again, when Lorette suddenly opened the front door.

She wore a completely transparent nightgown with a loose housecoat hanging from her shoulders.

The blood surged to her brow in a swift wave as she saw the direction of his glance, and then as he looked up, their eyes met and held, and for a long moment they were the only two people in the world, the only two living persons in a world that could have been so cold and grey and dead because of all that sundered them and kept them apart—and yet by some miracle was now glorious and glowing with grey and blue and silver and the sheen of frozen fire as the moonlight shone with an unearthly and mystic radiance and gave lift and meaning to everything, since they had been permitted to be here together, if only for a little while in the brief and cruel transience of time—to be with each other, the one understanding the other, always compassionate and sympathetic, helping and deriving comfort from each other. And in their understanding and their awareness of that communion of spirit there was now joy and happiness, wonder and thankfulness, and a great and abiding peace.

Her hair was tousled, her make-up a ruin. His eyes looked down again. He could not help himself. He looked down and the spell was broken.

Again the flush surged to her brow. Her eyes met his anxiously—and yet proudly and bravely.

'I—I did what you told me to do, M'sieu Pinaud. I took your advice. You were right and I was wrong. Thanks to you—because of what you told me—and what you did for me this evening, I have been given the chance to try again.'

There was a long silence.

She would never know, he thought dully. She would never know how much she was hurting him with every word. She might guess. She probably would guess. She was intelligent enough—and some things did not have to be put into words.

But she would never know the agonizing pain—the flooding and sickening and almost blinding hurt that his vivid and compelling imagination inflicted on his emotions and his senses with a savage violence that was almost physical in its intensity . . .

He could see them together. He could watch them and hear them, envy them and hate them—and still love her . . .

M. le Chef's voice, resonant and querulous, came from the stairs behind her.

'Well—don't stand there, Lorette, so that everyone can see. Bring him in and close the door.'

He came across the great hall behind her. He wore a silk dressing-gown with a flamboyant pattern and his hair was sticking up and out from his head. Beneath the hem of the robe his legs were thin and white, and his neck,

without its habitual encircling collar starched to an im-
maculate whiteness, looked thin and scrawny. He obviously wore no pyjamas.

M. Pinaud looked at him as Lorette stepped back and
he entered the house. He realized, with a feeling of shock
and revulsion, that he had deliberately and purposely put
M. le Chef out of his mind since his conversation with
Henri Bayard.

'Come on in, Pinaud.'

He saw the plaster on M. Pinaud's forehead.

'Are you all right?'

'Yes, thank you, m'sieu. I had a doctor in gaol.'

'Lorette told me what you did for her. We can never
thank you enough—but come on inside. I should think you
could use a drink.'

'I will go up, if you would please excuse me,' said
Lorette quietly. 'I am sure you have a lot to talk about.'

He watched her run up the stairs and did not see her.

'Thank you, m'sieu,' he said and sat down heavily in an
armchair, his mind not even hearing what he was saying,
but immersed in his own thoughts.

Why had he done that? Why had he deliberately closed
his mind to M. le Chef? Surely there could be no degrees,
no qualifications nor limitations in friendship. Nor in marriage, as he had tried to explain to Lorette. One had a
friend, one took a wife. For better or for worse. With all
their virtues and all their faults. Otherwise the words had
no meaning, the concept and the ideal no value.

On the other hand, the old man's story about his grand-
daughter's death had touched him deeply and affected him
profoundly, to a degree that the mental barrier had seemed
to descend of its own volition—in spite of him and not
because of him.

He became aware that M. le Chef was standing in front
of him and regarding him curiously. In his hand he held
a huge balloon glass almost filled with what looked like
brandy.

'What is the matter, Pinaud?' he asked quietly.

He took the glass and swallowed half its contents before
answering. It was brandy—an exceptionally good one. Then

he set the glass down carefully on a small table beside him and looked up directly at M. le Chef.

'I had a talk with Henri Bayard,' he said slowly. 'He told me about his grand-daughter Yvonne and how she died.'

There was a long silence after he had said this. The old house was utterly quiet. The log fire had died down to a few glowing embers.

M. le Chef's eyes seemed to turn inwards and he stayed completely still.

'What else did he tell you, Pinaud?' he asked. His voice was even quieter than before. It was less than a whisper. It was like the rustle of leaves blown in an autumn breeze.

M. Pinaud tried to answer and found that he had no words.

'Tell me. I have a right to know.'

'He said—he said that she was a good and innocent young girl—a virgin—and that you corrupted her and debauched her and drove her to suicide.'

There. That was over. Now he had said it he felt better. Now that the festering words were out from inside him perhaps the wound would heal. Subconsciously, they must have been tormenting him since he heard them. He looked at his glass and decided that he would not touch it.

Still M. le Chef had not moved. And yet, watching him closely, M. Pinaud realized that somehow, indefinably, he had gained a certain stature and dignity, in spite of his gown and his rumpled hair.

'I am sorry you should have heard this from him, Pinaud. And I am grateful to you for telling me.'

His voice was a little stronger now, but still quiet.

'I will tell you the truth. Yvonne Bayard was a nymphomaniac.'

For a moment M. Pinaud sat in a stunned silence. As always, when confronted with another example of human duplicity, he felt an emptiness, a sadness and a sense of shock and loss which seemed to diminish him because it diminished his faith in human beings.

He looked at his glass, reached out wordlessly and drained the other half of its contents in one gulp.

M. le Chef walked over to the cabinet by the wall and returned with the bottle of brandy. He refilled the glass and then stood there and addressed his words to the bottle in his hand. As he spoke, so his voice gathered strength and resonance and conviction, and beneath each word there vibrated an intensity and a sincerity that were utterly and completely convincing.

'She arrived here—out of the blue—with a letter of introduction from her grandfather. He obviously knew nothing about her. He felt he was doing his duty and discharging his obligations to her dead parents by writing it. Her father and mother had been local people. My family knew them well. The first night she was in the house I was working in my study when she called me. This was before I married Lorette and we were alone in the house. I went upstairs and found her in my bedroom, lying naked on her back on my bed.'

He stopped and looked at the bottle in his hand, as if wondering how it had got there. Then he placed it carefully on the small table beside M. Pinaud's glass and thrust his hands into the pockets of his dressing-gown as he continued.

'She was obviously a minor. I knew enough about the law not to touch her. I tried to tell her how she would end up—what her life would soon become if she went on like this—but I was wasting my breath. She was like a bitch in heat. I argued and pleaded, and lectured and threatened. It was like talking to a brick wall.'

For one brief instant a glint of the old humour seemed to bring his eyes alive.

'Well—not quite, perhaps. Because her only answer to everything I said was to open and spread her legs a little wider—and I am only human.

'I finally got out of the room—I don't know how—and slept on the sofa in my study, with the door locked. In the morning I left early. When I came home that evening I thought at first that she had left. I went up to her room to make sure and found her dead. She had taken an over-dose of barbiturates.'

M. Pinaud stirred in his chair.

'But why—'

'I don't know, Pinaud. To this day I don't know why. And it is not through lack of thinking about it, I can assure you. The only conclusion to which I can come is that when I was trying every possible argument to convince her I must have threatened to tell her grandfather, Henri Bayard. This is the only reason I can think of. She did not know me. And when I walked out and left her there she still did not know what I intended doing. She could not trust me not to tell him. Her whole life must have been a pretence with him, particularly after her parents were killed. Otherwise how could he have held that opinion of her? She probably could not face or even contemplate the thought of him knowing the truth about her.'

M. Pinaud moved again in his chair.

'And would you?' he asked quietly.

'Would I what?'

'Would you have told him?'

If there had been an indefinable dignity in M. le Chef's manner during this extraordinary recital, there was now a positive majesty in the simple words of his reply.

'Of course not, Pinaud. You know me better than that. I only mentioned it to her because I could think of nothing else to say. Henri Bayard is brave and honest and patriotic. He became a hero in the Resistance—an example which inspired thousands—and was decorated by de Gaulle. He is also a supremely religious and proud old man—I would have broken his heart.'

For a long moment there was silence.

'And yet, in consequence and as a result, he is convinced that you are a—'

'Let him be convinced, then,' interrupted M. le Chef suddenly and fiercely. 'What do I care? What does it matter? I can live with it. My conscience is clear. There was no alternative. I could not tell him the truth. I could not bring myself to destroy his ideals. Better he should live with hate in his heart than die of a broken one.'

M. Pinaud looked at his glass with approval. It was excellent brandy, and therefore an eminently suitable drink to use for such a fitting toast as the one he intended to propose, silently and secretly and sincerely.

What he had just heard pleased him. This was thinking and logic he could understand. These were principles and rules of conduct on which he had been brought up. Here he was on familiar and well-loved ground, after a nightmare of wandering blindly along unknown paths. This was the vindication of all his ideals and beliefs about friendship. This was his friend who had proved worthy of his trust. Surely, if ever there was a reason and an occasion for drinking, this was it.

He did so. He drank a silent and yet none the less sincere toast to friendship.

The brandy warmed his stomach, comforted his heart and sharpened his senses.

'Have you thought,' he said slowly, 'that he might have done this thing to you—this murder in your bed—out of revenge? For what he thinks you did to his grand-daughter?'

For a moment M. le Chef looked startled. Then he shook his head, decisively and with conviction.

'No.'

'Why not?'

'It is not his nature to kill. He is too religious.'

'He might—if he had enough provocation. He has killed and helped to kill before.'

'That was different. That was in the war—when all ideals and beliefs were suspended. To him, that was not killing, but extermination. He was fighting the anti-Christ.'

'He might have thought he was still doing that.'

'I can't believe it.'

'Why did he come here, then—to work for you?'

'Because Yvonne is buried here. He still prays for the child he once knew.'

Lorette came down the stairs. She had combed and brushed her hair and made up her face. She wore a long quilted and full-skirted housecoat, with a broad sash closely tied.

M. Pinaud started to get up but she raised her hand.

'No, please—stay there and enjoy your drink.'

She sat down in another chair.

'I will go up and get some clothes on,' announced M. le Chef suddenly. 'You will stay the night here, of course, Pinaud—the room is always ready.'

'Thank you, m'sieu. That is kind of you. I have to go out first, but I shall be pleased to accept later on.'

M. le Chef started to say something and then changed his mind.

'Good. Tomorrow we will sort out Inspector Salvan, with the help of Maître Mansard. By the way, you have not told us how you got out.'

'It was not very complicated, m'sieu. I jumped the man who brought my tray, tied him up and took his keys and gun. Then I persuaded the desk sergeant to join him in my cell and cut the telephone. They were the only two there.'

M. le Chef began to climb the stairs.

'I have often been thankful, Pinaud,' he said over his shoulder, 'that fate did not make you a criminal.'

Now when he had gone upstairs a constraint came between them, falling like a shadow, hanging like a shroud—invisible and intangible and yet palpable—a certainty of the imagination so intense that he felt as if his eyes could almost see it.

They sat there for a long time in silence before the dying fire.

M. Pinaud looked at his glass and the bottle.

'Can I get you a drink?' he asked quietly.

'No, thank you.'

She did not look at him as she replied.

He reached for his glass and as he drank slowly his mind raced with all his thoughts in chaotic confusion.

This was not what he had wanted to say. This was not what she had expected to hear—or else why had she refused? And why was she avoiding his eyes? Were his thoughts so obvious? That would explain this strange and almost frightening feeling of constraint, which had never existed before between them.

He drank again and then poured more brandy into his glass, very slowly and very carefully.

Better to drink than to talk, Pinaud, he told himself sternly. Think what you are doing. Be very careful. The things you want to say are best left unsaid.

This is the young and very lovely wife of your friend and your employer. You have had the audacity and the temerity to preach to her about marriage—your thoughts therefore are not only better left unsaid but in addition ought to be cleaned from your mind. You have been able to help her. Leave it at that. Be thankful you had the chance. Few people are so fortunate.

You only pass this way once. The opportunity to do any good thing is so rare as to be priceless, because you will not pass this way again. Finish what you began. Stop lusting after her body. Give her some more good advice, and then get out and leave her alone. She has found enough complications in this marriage of hers without your adding to them.

He looked at her with tenderness, understanding and compassion and saw that there were tears in her eyes.

'What is it, Lorette?' he asked very gently.

Still she would not look at him as she answered.

'I have hurt you—I have been so thoughtless—'

'No.'

Tell her anything—lie to her if necessary—rather than watch her cry.

'I have—I know. After all you have done for me—'

He stood up in one swift movement and placed a hand, with infinite gentleness, on her shoulder.

'I did what anyone would have done. There is no need to cry.'

'I have been so foolish—so young. I should have known —I ought to have realized—'

Now she turned her head and looked directly at him.

'I always seem to be doing the wrong thing, don't I? At least I should have waited until I had shown my gratitude to you—and then perhaps it would have been different—'

'Different, maybe—but not better. I gave you some good

advice, and you were wise enough to take it. That is all. There is nothing else.'

There could be nothing else, he told himself fiercely. There must be nothing else. Remember your feelings when you heard about him and Yvonne Bayard. Imagine what his would be when he learnt that you had made love to his wife.

'Is that what you want?'

The blue eyes seemed to be piercing the shadows—and the dimness and the moisture behind his own—with the blue light that had once been in the moonlight, with the blue shade of gentian in the sun . . .

In spite of himself his hand tightened convulsively— with sudden and frightening strength—on her shoulder. He felt like shouting and screaming a denial.

He heard her quick gasp of pain, loosened his grip and stepped back away from her chair.

'No,' he said quietly. 'You and I both know the truth. That is not what I want. It is not what you want either. But that is what it is going to be.'

He turned towards the small table, took up his glass and drank its contents quickly, resisting a stupid and yet almost overwhelming desire to put the neck of the bottle in his mouth and swallow until it was empty.

'Look, Lorette,' he said, speaking quietly and quickly. 'There is not much time. I have to go out as soon as your husband comes down. I gave you some advice this morning. May I give you a little more?'

'Of course.'

'I have a great admiration for your uncle, the Duke. He is a powerful and influential man. Power and influence are supposed to corrupt. I would not say that this has been true in his case, but they are bound to have some effect on him. One cannot expect him, in his position, to accept the standard limitations of conduct imposed on other men. His decisions would never be influenced by all those considerations which always affect ours.'

'What do you mean?' she whispered, suddenly pitifully tense.

'It is always dangerous for a man to play God. For your own sake you must not get too close to him. You are too much engrossed in your family. You have reason enough to be proud of it—but when you marry you should both create a new and independent life—you and your husband are the only two who can live it. Marriage must be the final severance of the cord, if only as an act of faith in your husband. You have never cut it, Lorette. This will take courage—but I know you have enough to do it.'

She stared at him, her eyes wide with sudden awareness and a growing fear.

"What—what are you trying to tell me?' she whispered.

M. le Chef came down the stairs. He had put on a shirt, slacks and a pullover, and had combed and brushed his hair.

'Sorry to be so long,' he said cheerfully. 'What about something to eat—you must be starving, Pinaud.'

Then his shrewd eyes narrowed as he looked from one to the other, sensing at once the constraint between them.

'What is the matter?' he asked quietly.

Lorette stood up and spoke with complete self-possession.

'Of course he is starving. Of course he should rest—he has been hurt because of me. But you heard him before you went up. He says he has to go out.'

M. le Chef turned, but M. Pinaud was already halfway to the door.

'But—'

'I shall not be long. Tell you all about it when I come back.'

And he left them alone, closing the front door quietly behind him.

12

He walked away from the house to the parkland, tranquil and grey in the light of the moon.

He had to get away. He had to get out of that house and away from both of them. That was why he had said that he had to go out. He had to be alone for a while with his thoughts.

Then he stopped, lit a cigarette and forced himself to think rationally.

Your mind, Pinaud, he told himself sternly, is confused with emotion, when all it needs is logic. You have allowed yourself to come too near and too close to these people, to become too emotionally involved even to think clearly.

She is not only your employer's young and lovely wife, after whose body you are lusting—she is a suspect. She could easily have done it. She left Charanton in time to arrive while he was out. She had a key. She could have gone straight up to the bedroom. The housemaid might even have been asleep, unaware of the door opening. Her uncle said she had a wild streak in her. The tyre-lever was kept on the floor of her car. She could have run down the stairs quickly and quietly to get it, and then, mad with childish and wanton rage and hate and jealousy—she is still a suspect, Pinaud, whatever your dreams and desires and emotions are trying to tell you.

The trees and bushes were black in the distant shadows, silver and grey around him, the turf and grass a sea of frozen white foam. The whole world slept as the moon rode high and proud in the sky.

And Henri Bayard. M. le Chef was quite convinced and certain and positive that he is innocent. But the arguments you gave him a little while ago were good ones and still valid, and if you remember—now that your brain is at last beginning to function normally—he did not refute them. He avoided them. He skated around them.

Of course Bayard would come to Pontlieu if his grand-daughter were buried here—what more fitting locale could he find in which to consummate his revenge? Too religious to kill—that was nonsense. How much blood had been shed in the name of religion since the world began? He had killed before—he could have killed again. And to him this would not have been killing, but extermination. If the soldiers—obeying orders—who had occupied his country were the anti-Christ, what was the man who debauched his grand-daughter and drove her to suicide?

Your arguments, Pinaud, had been sound and logical and valid—why were they not followed up? Because Lorette had come into the room and you ceased to be a detective and became a love-sick boy. Now you are alone. Now you can use your brain and think. Henri Bayard is still a suspect. The most likely one too, because of his very nature, because of his exploits during the occupation and because—not in spite—of his religion.

And since at last you are being logical, you should not leave out the Duke. When you tried to warn Lorette just now her reactions surprised you. Perhaps there has been some trouble before of a similar kind—trouble which money and influence could so easily suppress.

A man still living—incredibly and anachronistically—in a feudal state in this twentieth century, surrounded by people conditioned to a tradition of loyalty and implicit obedience by generations of consistent upbringing—what if he had seen in this situation an opportunity to end a marriage which had only brought disillusion and misery to the happy niece he remembered? The order would have been given and the order would have been obeyed, quickly and efficiently and without question. With absolute power he would not need to soil his own hands.

The Duke of Charanton—suspect for murder. He may be on your list, Pinaud, but that is one you will never prove. You can question his retainers until you are black in the face and they will lie for him as they have been taught to lie at their fathers' knees, and he will produce alibis and witnesses to prove that their lies are the truth,

which is his part of the protection they have been brought
up to expect as their right—part of the bargain and the
fealty and the covenant. And you will look a fool.

Each leaf and branch had a radiance, a beauty and a
magic the moonbeams enfolded. Each tall tree-trunk, in its
garment of blue and silver, seemed striving to reach the
moon, knowing and questing for the source of the light.
The world around him was empty and he suddenly felt
utterly alone and lonely and afraid.

He would go to M. Poidevin and talk things over with
him.

Once before—so many years ago—he had been lonely
and unhappy, confused and afraid, and from the older
man's sympathy and encouragement and help he had found
comfort and courage to go on. There came a time when
the burden seemed too heavy to bear alone, the odds too
great to fight, the decisions too momentous to attempt alone.
There was a time when the mere act of talking released the
pent-up tensions and the sound of the thoughts becoming
words provided the ease and the anodyne and the comfort
for the pain.

This was the time, then. The house was not far.

M. Poidevin's eyes widened in surprise but there was no
hesitation in the urbane voice as he stepped back and held
the door wide.

'Why Pinaud—what brings you here? Come in. Come
inside.'

'Thank you, m'sieu. You will forgive me for calling like
this, but I felt I would like to talk to you.'

'Of course—why not? Here—come in here.'

M. Pinaud followed him into the room in which they
had sat before. The lights were not on and the wide heavy
curtains were drawn back. Behind the glass the unfinished
garden seemed to glow in the grey and almost incandescent
sheen of the moonlight.

M. Poidevin's hand was already outstretched to the
switch when M. Pinaud's voice arrested him.

'No, please—don't turn them on, m'sieu. That is, if you

have no objection. I have just walked through the park—
the moonlight is so beautiful—'

'Yes. I can imagine. I was sitting here in the dark,
watching it, when you rang the bell.'

M. Pinaud walked across the room and stood in front
of the window, looking out.

'Well,' M. Poidevin continued, still standing in the doorway, 'the coffee is hot on the stove and although the night
is clear, it has turned colder. Therefore with the coffee I
would recommend a large glass of brandy, in case you
may have caught a chill.'

'You are very kind, m'sieu.'

He heard a voice saying the words and he swung around,
because he knew that he did not mean them, that it could
not have been he who had spoken, because he would never
have said them.

But M. Poidevin was already in the kitchen. The door
was open and he was alone in the room.

He turned back to the window, looked intently out
through the glass panes at the unfinished garden. He had
been staring out like this when he had spoken, automatically
and mechanically, and at the same instant a sudden thought
had pierced through his mind with the sharpness of a sword.

He had been standing there in the same place, earlier on
that evening, watching a young man shovelling earth in the
clear bright light of the sun. At the time he watched he had
felt that something was wrong, but he could not decide
what it was.

Now he remembered. Now in retrospect he saw the whole
scene again. And now he knew.

There were so many things about which he knew nothing.
But quite a number about which he knew a little. Gardening
was one of them. He knew how to shovel loose earth—the
knee is pressed against the back of the hand for leverage, to
give the power for the shovel to enter deeply enough into
the loose earth to be filled. The young man shovelling—
supposed to be a gardener—did not know this. A real
gardener would have known. A thug, hired to play the part
of a gardener, would not have known, nor would he have
cared.

A second thought flashed behind the first, with that instantaneous wonder which is the miracle of perception. Although it had been too far to distinguish his features, the clothes had been the same—heavy boots, dirty jeans and a dirty T-shirt. And the hair had been long.

Then the second thought dissolved instantaneously into a third. All his other suspects knew about M. le Chef's evening walk. But a man who had just moved into the neighbourhood would not have known. Therefore he would have asked him to come over, on some pretext of asking his advice about the garden to ensure that he was out of the house last night.

And the fourth and last thought pierced his mind as M. Poidevin entered the room carrying a tray in one hand. It was strange that he should have come to this remote part of the country to retire, just because a friend lived near, when he had a son, of whom he was very fond, living in the south.

'May I put on the light?' asked M. Poidevin from the doorway. 'This brandy is too good to spill—'

'Of course.'

M. Poidevin touched a switch and the room was flooded with light. He moved across the floor to put the tray down on the sideboard. M. Pinaud walked past him to the door.

Now all the thoughts had coalesced in his mind to make one vivid picture. Now he knew the truth. The gaoler's gun was suddenly in his hand, and his voice was hard and cold.

'I am sorry you went to all this trouble. I shall not drink it.'

Nothing could shake the man's composure. Deliberately he turned his back on the gun and spoke over his shoulder as he walked to the window.

'At least let me pull the curtains, now that the light is on.'

M. Pinaud did not answer. M. Poidevin drew the curtains. Then he sat down, crossed his legs and lit a cigarette. He was perfectly calm, poised and assured. M. Pinaud remained standing by the door.

'The coffee is poured and the brandy in the glasses—do help yourself.'

'No, thank you.'

The ironic smile touched the corners of that mobile mouth.

'At least—sit down and put that gun away. I am un-armed. Physically I am no match for you. And you know I hate violence.'

M. Pinaud continued to stand and hold the gun.

'And yet you deal in it.'

'Sometimes one has to use the only tools available.'

'You are surprised to see me, m'sieu?'

'Of course.'

"Because no doubt Inspector Salvan informed you that I was safely locked up.'

'I don't know what you are talking about.'

'I think you do. M'sieu Poidevin—let us drop this farce. Your three thugs are out of action, but you are surprised because you did not think that you would need them any more tonight. That is why I broke out of the gaol and came here.'

For a long moment there was silence. Then M. Poidevin ground out his cigarette in an ash-tray, shrugged and smiled.

'Pinaud,' he said quietly. 'You really are incredible. You always have been. You walk out of a locked and bolted prison, guarded by two armed men—just like that. When I opened the door to you this morning I knew that it was all over.'

He sighed and then shrugged again.

'Tell me one thing—how did you know?'

M. Pinaud did not relax.

'Your thug I saw from this window was not a gardener. He did not know how to dig. And it was a mistake to send him and the others to beat me up and put me out of the way in broad daylight. He seemed vaguely familiar. I remembered just now, looking out of that window, where I had seen him before. And one or two small things. You were the only one who did not know of M. le Chef's evening walk. You had to ask him to come over here to give your thug with the hammer time to get into the manor-house.'

Again there was a long moment of silence. Then M. Poidevin spread his long-fingered hands in a gesture of resignation that seemed incongruously pathetic. For a moment he paused and seemed to collect and marshal his thoughts. Then he spoke again, even more quietly.

'Very well, Pinaud. I could make a speech filled with sentimental slush—about a young man with ideals who once took public office with the quaint and mediaeval idea that in it he would live by his principles. And how over the years he watched both his principles and his ideals die—suffocated in a swamp of corruption. But that would be both pointless and a waste of time. Let us just say that I have grown old and tired and I chose—quite deliberately—the easy way and the money.'

He sat up straight in the chair and placed his hands on his knees.

'I told you something about the organization in Nice and Marseilles. The plans were to expand in Paris. Therefore your employer, who—largely thanks to you and your efforts —has proved himself a nuisance, had to be removed.'

M. Pinaud looked down at the gun as if he saw it for the first time, but the hand that held it remained as steady as a rock.

'I find it hard to believe,' he heard his own voice saying, 'as hard and as strange as accepting the fact that a trust can be betrayed.'

He shivered suddenly, although the room was warm. He shivered as if with cold and continued to listen to what his own voice was saying, speaking the words not only to the man in front of him but to himself as well.

'The world must indeed be sick today if it can poison men like you, m'sieu. You are prepared to let an innocent man —your own friend—rot in prison for a crime he did not commit. You were prepared to kill a girl you did not even know—and you did not have the courage to do it yourself, but paid your thug with a hammer to do it for you. For what? For money.'

He paused for a moment, and then as he continued, his voice, which had been biting with scorn and contempt, grew softer and quieter.

'I find this hard to accept. As hard as I find it to pull this trigger and kill you myself.'

M. Poidevin said something, but he did not hear the words. He heard instead the same voice saying other words —words this man had said to him, many years ago, when he had gone, young and proud and confident, to that beautiful stone house in the Ile de France to ask for his help. While there are men like you, Pinaud, doing their duty, unafraid and incorruptible, there is still hope for France.

The world then—with all its faults—must have been a far cleaner place.

M. Poidevin's face was white. His eyes shifted restlessly, almost wildly, but always came back to the gun in M. Pinaud's hand.

'I could disappear—quietly somewhere—not bother any-one—'

In spite of himself M. Pinaud could not keep the bitter-ness out of his voice as he interrupted.

'Yes—you have made enough money, I suppose, to make such an operation a simple one. That would be the easy way.'

Then he shook his head, and in his voice anger burnt out the bitterness like a flame consumes straw.

'No, m'sieu—why should you have the easy way out? I will give you an alternative.'

'Why?'

Now the anger had gone, the flames burnt out. The bitterness and scorn belonged to another person. He spoke slowly and heavily, choosing his words with care.

'I think there must be three reasons. Because of all that you once did to help me, when I asked for your help. You gave me the strength and the courage to go on. I was young then and needed the advice and reassurance and encourage-ment which you gave so generously and ungrudgingly. That I can never forget.

'And secondly, because of the issues at stake.'

'What do you mean by that?' asked M. Poidevin slowly.

'Don't you see? Can't you understand? The hopes and the fears and the dreams of the small man—the average man—who can measure them? They are boundless, because

they are so simple—the wish to live his own life in peace
under the protection of a law that is above corruption—and
the rightful ambition to bring up his children in honesty and
decency—is that too much to expect? But you and your
kind are out to corrupt the only people in whom he can
put his trust—the very people on whom he relies to enforce
that law which is his only hope.

'These things I see as of far greater importance than the
crime and punishment of one man.

'And lastly, because you are the only man who could do
what has to be done.'

'You mean—'

'Of course. Go back and fight, M'sieu Poidevin—as you
used to fight when I first knew you—as you have been
fighting all your life. As you fought when the world was a
cleaner place. This is the chance in a thousand—that very
few men get. We all make mistakes—how many of us get
the opportunity to put them right?'

M. Poidevin shook his head.

'I am too old—'

'Nonsense. You have the influence and the power and
the experience—get back in office and use them. Get the
army to help, if necessary—you will find there are still
generals and marshals who will be on your side. Expose and
stop the rot at the top—tear up the stones and let the
newspapers tell the people what is underneath. Get M'sieu
le Chef back where he belongs. You can rely on him. He
has his faults, but he is incorruptible—like you yourself
were once, m'sieu.'

M. Poidevin stirred in his chair.

'Like you are now Pinaud,' he said softly.

'I try to be. I like to sleep at night. There are so many
things in this life more important still than money, in spite
of our civilization which has made it into a god.'

There was a long and heavy silence, vaguely menacing in
its intensity.

M. Pinaud laid the gun down on a chair. Almost in the
same movement, it seemed, the other one he had taken
from the sergeant was in his hand. M. Poidevin did not
move.

'I ask you, m'sieu, to think about what I have said. I will wait outside to give you time.'

Then he went out, closing the door quietly behind him.

In the hall he felt stifled, so he opened the front door and waited outside.

The moonlight bathed and flooded everything with an unearthly and magical radiance. Behind him was no longer a house but the mediaeval barn that once had stood there when the world was young and a simpler and cleaner place.

In the moonlight he waited. In the bright and lovely light of the moon he forced himself to wait.

He felt suddenly tired and exhausted. His arm had started to throb and hurt and his head was aching. He was drained of all vitality. He felt like a psychiatrist who after hours of patient questioning had finally uncovered the cause of his patient's trauma, like a surgeon after a difficult and protracted operation, like a priest after the confessional. He had given of himself—to the uttermost.

It seemed—in that moment of loneliness and introspection—that all his life he had been waiting for things which did not happen.

There had been rare and wonderful exceptions—his wife's head on the pillow on their wedding night, the laughter and the sleeping tranquility of his children, praise from M. le Chef after an exceptionally difficult case—but always he had expected more, always he had waited for the perfection his imagination could so easily visualize.

This past day and night he had been waiting too—but now that was all over. It was better this way—far better the dream should have been broken and crushed before it grew wings to fly into reality.

If M. Poidevin made the right decision, then M. le Chef could expect the greatest test a man had ever known—at such a time he would need a loving and faithful wife. M. Poidevin would go unpunished, but the ultimate good he might achieve—which with his qualifications and his capabilities he would undoubtedly achieve—would surely weigh down the balance. The thug with the hammer who had actually committed the murder for money would be charged, once they had got rid of Inspector Salvan.

He waited in the moonlight, alone with his thoughts. It seemed to him in this vigil, sanctified by the peace and tranquility and the breathtaking beauty of the night, that he had always been waiting, all his life, for so much—

The shot rang out, sharp and sudden and clear, shattering the silence that had spread around him like a benediction.

The great trees of the parkland swept up the sound and smothered it, compressed the open wound and healed it, closed the rift and engulfed it with the slumbrous peace of their softly sighing branches.

M. Poidevin had chosen an even easier way. There was no need to look, no need to check. With his habitual efficiency, he would have placed the barrel in his mouth, pointing upwards, to ensure that the bullet pierced his brain.

Now the friendship was ended, the trust betrayed, the memory warped and belittled by bitterness.

He shivered suddenly. The coldness was not in the air but in his heart. He had hoped for too much. His had been the expectation of a visionary, an idealist and a perfectionist.

But surely it was better to fail a thousand times and to go on trying. Surely it was not unworthy to hope, to dream, to pray for the best and to believe in the best and to go on believing with that conviction and sincerity which always gave him the courage to try again . . .

He sighed and began to walk back towards the manor-house, sad with his thoughts of the pity and the tragedy, the horror and the waste of it all. He walked slowly and heavily, the moonlight glistening on the tears in his eyes.